"Are you in bed?"

Mary's middle-of-the-night laughter was low and throaty, and sent unexpected delight shooting through Michael. "No," she said, "but I'm close to it. I'm sitting on the blue chaise in my bedroom."

"What do you have on?"

"Michael!"

"You're naked?"

"Of course not. It's just such a—"

"A personal question. Yeah, but when I get a phone call at three in the morning, I figure I can take certain liberties."

Mary was smiling. There was something lovely about having Mike on the end of the phone line, as close to her as a heartbeat.... His voice was losing the sleepy tones, but she could still picture him there in his bed, his midnight blue eyes trying to focus, his chin covered with the shadow of a night's beard. She wondered what *he* had on, but she was afraid to ask....

ABOUT THE AUTHOR

Molly McGuire is the pseudonym of well-known romance writer Sally Goldenbaum. While Sally is the author of a number of romances, *Forever Yours* is her first book for Harlequin. She has been a teacher at both the high school and college levels, as well as a textbook writer and a public-relations writer for public television. Born in Wisconsin, Sally now lives in Kansas.

MOLLY McGUIRE

FOREVER YOURS

Harlequin Books

TORONTO • NEW YORK • LONDON
AMSTERDAM • PARIS • SYDNEY • HAMBURG
STOCKHOLM • ATHENS • TOKYO • MILAN
MADRID • WARSAW • BUDAPEST • AUCKLAND

Published April 1992

ISBN 0-373-16436-X

FOREVER YOURS

Printed in U.S.A.

Chapter One

Mary Shields stood in front of the dryer and watched the long-legged man across the room. He was sound asleep, with one arm curled beneath his head as a makeshift pillow and his legs bent to fit on the bench. He had been that way for the entire time she had been in Jake's Laundromat and that was going on two hours now. Several people had said hello to him as they passed by the sleeping form on their way to the detergent canteen and the rack of frayed magazines, but the man never moved or responded.

Mary looked at him closely as she pushed her rickety basket of clothes over to a folding table. She did not know him, but that was hardly earthshaking. She had not yet met many people in the small Indiana college town—some faculty members connected to the writers' workshop, a nice woman in the administration offices, but that was nearly it.

She absently folded a pair of blue jeans and thought about being alone here for twelve weeks, of teaching, of meeting the bright young people who were fortunate and talented enough to be admitted to the prestigious writing program. It would be a lonely time for her. She knew she'd miss New York terribly, but the challenge of teaching was exciting. The newness of the situation, even being alone, should appeal to her as a writer. She should explore the emotion, ponder the thin rivers of loneliness that passed through her, and then put it down on paper. But loneliness wasn't something that particularly interested Mary's creative mind, perhaps because she'd lived so many years of it.

Besides, tonight she was too tired to ponder. She envied the sleeping man across the room, for she hadn't slept well since her arrival in Chestershire. It was the newness, she told herself. The strange bed. The water. The anxiety. And the man across the room from her was probably a lifelong resident who suffered from none of these things, and that was why he could sleep like a baby on the hard wooden bench.

The man stirred then and Mary leaned on her elbows at the Formica folding table and watched his lips curve into a smile. The smile changed his face, softening his angular features and heightening the five-o'clock shadow on his square chin. He must be dreaming, she thought. Nice.

She wondered why the slapping whir of the washing machines and the constant buzz of the dryers did not wake him. Square metal baskets screeched by, just inches from his face, but he never moved.

"Hi."

Mary's head snapped up.

It was not until the deep voice registered over her thoughts that she realized she had stopped seeing the man for a moment while her mind played on with its own images. She quickly focused on the person behind the voice. His eyes were open now and he was looking directly at her.

"I'm Mike Gibson," he said pleasantly. "How do you like me so far?"

There was no arrogance in his tone, only a touch of humor. Mary laughed, a short, nervous laugh, and then fidgeted with the brown T-shirt she was folding until it resembled a mound of chunky peanut butter. "I'm sorry for staring. My mind was elsewhere."

"And that makes *me* sorry," Mike Gibson said. The smile that followed his words formed a large indentation in one cheek and Mary's gaze focused on it rather than on the eyes that seemed to see into her in a way that made her uncomfortable. "How do you sleep like that?" she asked.

"Was I snoring?"

"No, I mean in the middle of all the commotion. This isn't your normal bed-and-breakfast. And that bench looks dreadfully hard."

"I've slept on worse." He swung his legs around until his large feet landed on the floor and his torso was upright. When he stretched his arms to squeeze away the last remnants of sleep, Mary noticed the worn T-shirt that he wore. CHESTERSHIRE COLLEGE was printed across the front in faded blue letters. "Oh, you're at the college," she said.

"That I am. And you? I don't think I've seen you around here before."

Mary smiled. She felt more comfortable talking to him now that there was a connection. She wished she felt less leery of strangers, but it was difficult to put aside the careful training of twenty-nine years. So she still approached new faces carefully, with some restraint and hesitation. "I'm at the college, too," she said. "I arrived a short while ago, so you're right, you probably haven't seen me before."

"Student?" Mike lifted one thick brown as he took in her slender figure and the thick black hair that fell in unruly waves to her shoulders. There was a young blush about her and an incredibly youthful vibrancy and anticipation in her smile, but the expression in her eyes contradicted it all. It was old, mixed with young; a life already lived wedged in tightly beside the glow of expectation.

Mary straightened beneath his scrutiny. "No, I'm with the writers' workshop here," she said. "Teaching." The words were said with some pride and Mary heard it in her own voice. *Deserved* pride, she thought. Chestershire College was famous for its workshop and being invited to sit on the faculty for a session was a feather in any writer's literary cap. It was a quiet compliment, an acknowledgment of one's work, and Mary was determined to milk it for all it was worth, even if she were a last-minute replacement for a better-known novelist who had taken ill.

"Good for you," Mike said, with a slight nod of his head.

"I'm looking forward to it. It will be good for my career."

Mike looked at her as she said the words and recognized the ambition in the slender woman with the shy smile. There was definitely more there than had met his first sleepy glance.

He stood and Mary straightened to her full height as he moved, then found herself looking up into his face. He had not looked so tall when he was curled up on the bench, nor so interesting. Faint laugh lines around his eyes told her he was older than she was. Six or seven years would be her guess. And beneath the power of his gaze was a kindness that made her think of a man who probably shoveled snow for old ladies and had a big shaggy dog. Or maybe children. And pain. There was some pain in Mike Gibson's clear blue gaze.

"Are you married?" Mary's words came out without warning.

Mike saw her discomfiture and held back his smile. "No. Are you?"

Mary's fingers looped a pair of socks together. "No," she said.

"Well, good. Let's go for it then."

Mary looked up, startled, and then saw in his eyes that he was teasing her again. She lifted one shoulder and grinned. "Sorry for being so personal. I guess watching you sleep made me think I knew you."

"That's fine with me. How about if we pull out all the stops and really do it right? What's your name?" Mike flipped up the lid of a washer while he talked.

Mary's laughter came more quickly this time. She felt a strain lift from her shoulders and a nice warm trickle run through her center. "Mary. Mary Shields. Nice to meet you, Mike."

She turned and opened the door to the now quiet dryer and pulled the warm clothing out into her basket.

Opposite her, Mike tugged on damp flattened pieces of material in the washer and dropped them into a wicker basket. "All right, Mary Shields," he said as he worked, "I'm going to push the intimacy of this new relationship to its outer limits. Can you handle it?"

Mary shoved her hands into the pockets of her jeans and smiled at him. She liked this Mike. She liked the way he made her feel. "Try me."

"How about letting me dump my duds in your warm dryer?" One shaggy brow lifted again over clear blue laughing eyes.

Mary frowned sternly. "That's a toughie. My father always taught me six months, at least, before sharing dryers."

"Sh-h-h," Mike said, holding up one hand and briefly brushing her lips with his fingers. "Fathers don't need to know everything. Trust me, Mary Shields."

When he removed his fingers from her lips, the warm, tingling press of them remained. Strange, Mary thought, but very nice. She tucked away the feeling to be analyzed later.

She continued to watch him as he dumped the small armful of clothes into the belly of the dryer and then shoved a coin through the slot with strong, blunt fingers. His faded jeans fit tightly on a frame that, while not massive, showed athletic strength. Speckles of white paint were drizzled across the rear pocket and down one side. Somehow it looked natural and right on him, not messy, and Mary wondered if perhaps he were an artist.

Mike turned around. "And now, Mary, for your graciousness, I have a treat—"

Before Mary could answer he had returned to the bench and picked up a bulging backpack. "We have here savory delights that will knock your socks off. It's an old family recipe."

Mary circled the table and sat down on the bench beside him. The strange meeting with this friendly Chestershire man was washing her tiredness away and she suddenly realized she was hungry. Eating alone was a chore, so Mary had skipped dinner, and lunch had been a piece of fruit and a candy bar from a machine. She was more than hungry; she was starved. "What's in there?"

"Patience, my friend." Mike stuck one hand into the canvas bag and pulled out a foil-wrapped package, then another, and finally two bottles of beer.

"Do you do this regularly? Pick up women in the Laundromat, I mean, and then feed them?"

"Absolutely not. I don't usually share." He began unwrapping one of the sandwiches and set it in Mary's lap. "Consider yourself lucky, Mary."

Mary eyed the thick, juicy sandwich, then picked it up eagerly and took a bite.

Mike watched her carefully. Then he grinned. "I know, incredible isn't it?"

Mary wiped a dollop of mustard from the corner of her mouth. "You're not very modest, but you're right. It's great. What is it?"

"I can't tell you that. But folks have been known to wander in off the streets for it, so be careful." He picked up his own portion. Tiny sunflower seeds fell to the floor.

Mary took a drink of beer and leaned back against the bench. "Do you come here often, Mike?"

"No. Damn dryer blew up yesterday. I'm supposed to know how to fix things, but the more I tinkered, the more parts ended up on the floor."

Mary laughed. "You live alone?"

A gust of air blew her words away and she and Mike looked up as two young people in Chestershire sweatshirts entered the Laundromat. Mike waved a greeting and the couple walked over to where Mary and Mike were sitting.

"Ted and Diana," Mike said, "meet Mary Shields. Mary is with the writers' workshop."

"Of course she is," Diana said with some awe. She held out her hand to Mary. *"Gideon's Gambit,"* she announced proudly. "What a pleasure to meet you, Miss Shields."

Mary's smile stretched from one side of her face to the other. "You've read my book?" Her heart was beating rapidly. It would surprise and delight her as long as she lived, she thought, that perfect strangers would reach out to her, feel they knew her somehow, because they had read something she had written.

"I've read every single word. Twice," Diana added, with slight breathlessness.

Mike watched the exchange and was suddenly happy he had met Mary in a plain and simple way, without having to wade through what others knew or thought about her. In California, people always asked "What do you do?," right off the bat, as if that somehow defined a person. "So," he said now, his eyes turning to Mary, "My new friend is famous and she never said a word."

Mary opened her mouth to speak but Diana interrupted, as if Mary were not there. "Mary Shields is an exciting new novelist. Why, her picture was in *Vanity Fair,* right next to Jessica Lange and Sam Shepard! They were probably considering the screen rights to her book. They were sitting there in a restaurant, eating and talking—"

"Along with about fifteen others," Mary murmured beneath her breath. She had not been with the celebrities' party, nor had she ever met them before, but the reporter needed more people in the shot, and she knew one of the photographers, and her agent—

with whom she was dining at the time—knew the reporter, so she was it, an extra, so to speak. She was proud of the shot, anyway, because some day, as sure as she breathed, it would be *her* name in bold print beneath the picture and the others would be the awed ones, thrilled to be in her presence.

Mike watched the thoughts flit across her face. He watched expressions studiously these days, committing them to the safest part of his memory, but he couldn't quite decode all of Mary Shields's. "Well, this is good to know," he said. "Next time I'll bring my autograph book," he said.

Mary only laughed. Diana went on. "I'm going to be in the workshop this semester, and I think I got the last spot in your class, Ms. Shields."

"Well, good, Diana," Mary said. "Then we'll be seeing a lot of each other."

Mike listened with half an ear. The remnant of the conversation that stayed with him was the "seeing a lot of Mary" part. There was something about the thought that brought pleasure to him. Mary Shields intrigued him, like an intricate machine whose parts he needed to figure out. And he liked the fact that she'd only be there for the semester because that created a built-in protection against a messy entanglement in which someone would get hurt. He could simply enjoy the brief friendship. Southern Indiana autumns were known for their exciting beauty; Mary Shields made him think this one might be spectacular.

He focused back on Mary. The students had moved on to an empty washing machine and Mary was efficiently folding her clothes into a plastic basket. "You're leaving, Mary?"

"Yes, I am. I'm finished." She reached out and touched his arm. "And thanks to you, my hunger, as well as my wash, is taken care of, and I've met nice people, besides." She rolled a towel up and tucked it into the side of her hamper, then looked back at Mike. "You've turned a tedious night into a very nice one, Mike. Thank you—"

"Listen, Mary, it was my pleasure. You're a wonderful dryer partner, really—the best I've had in a long time."

Mary laughed again and the laughter echoed the happy feelings washing through her body. It had been a nice night, indeed. Chestershire had been transformed from a cold midwestern college town to a warm and friendly place, and all in the space of three loads of wash.

SLEEP CAME EASILY. After a long bath in the claw-foot tub, Mary pulled on a fleecy gown, opened both windows in her tiny bedroom and snuggled down beneath the clean-smelling sheets and a heavy blue blanket.

As always, thoughts of her latest unfinished book filled her mind, but tonight the ideas only floated loosely about, like fluffy fragments of a cloud. What took form and later filled her dreams instead was the image of a tall, lanky man with a crooked smile, eating the biggest sandwich Mary had ever seen.

Hours later, sunshine poured in the open window and tugged Mary free of the best sleep she had had in weeks. She slipped out of bed and into a huge terry-cloth robe and padded softly into the small, efficient kitchen. It was amazing, she thought drowsily, how different things seemed today. The striped green curtains above the sink had looked dingy yesterday, but today they were soaked in sunshine and floated cheerfully over the wooden sill. She plugged in the coffeepot and busied herself in the cupboard while the slow familiar gurgle sang in the background. The dark brew smelled wonderful, delicious. She wrapped her arms around herself and smiled at the cool, dusty stripes of sunlight. Little Mary Sunshine, that's who she felt like. Corny, she thought. Very corny. The thought made her laugh out loud, and then she jumped as her laugh collided with the sudden ring of the doorbell.

It was an unwelcome sound in the soft symphony of morning noises and for a brief moment Mary thought she'd protest its intrusion by refusing to answer it. Then she just as quickly brushed away the dreamy, unreasonable emotion, walked to the front door and pulled it open.

Mike stood there, tall and quiet, his tennis shoes planted a foot apart, a brown paper sack tucked beneath one arm. "Hi," he said.

Mary fingered the sash on her robe. "Hi, yourself." And then she smiled, giving in to the unexpected pleasure that seeing him brought.

"Sorry to barge in like this." His words came out slowly. This was crazy. He wasn't uncomfortable— Mike was rarely uncomfortable—but he was surprised that seeing Mary again brought such nice feelings along with it and the surprise distracted him.

Mary looked at him carefully in the clean light of morning. It only confirmed what the fluorescent glare of the Laundromat had already told her: Mike Gibson was one fine specimen of a man. Reluctantly she pulled her gaze away from his body and concentrated on the brown paper bag that was wedged beneath his arm. She laughed lightly. "Thanks, anyway, Mike, but I couldn't."

"What?"

She nodded toward the sack. "The bag. The sandwich. Last night's dinner was the best I've had in weeks, but I don't think I could handle it for breakfast. I'm absolutely religious about starting my day with coffee and bagels."

"Oh, this." Mike glanced at the bag and smiled. "No, this isn't food. This belongs to you." He handed the bag to her.

Mary lifted the feathery light parcel. "Mine?"

"Well, yes. It seems I inadvertently confiscated—"

Mary's curiosity beat his explanation and she dipped into the bag to pull out the contents. Two filmy bras and a pair of lace panties dangled from her fingertips.

"Good morning, Mary."

Mary's eyes followed the voice and settled on the figure of a short, stocky man standing just a few yards beyond Mike. It was old Professor Atwood, the founding father of the writing workshop. He stood at the end of her walkway, staring curiously at her and Mike. Milton, his faithful sheepdog, stood patiently at his side.

"Professor—"

Mike turned around. "Oh, hi, Professor Atwood."

"Well, hello, Michael," Professor Atwood said cheerfully. "I see you two have met. Wonderful. Michael is a good person to know around here, Mary. He's a genius. He—" His words fell off as he stared openly at Mary's outstretched hand.

Mary's eyes widened as her cheeks began a slow burn. "I, oh, well, yes, you're right about Mike. And we did meet, at the dryer—"

The professor's bushy white brows lifted.

"Last night," Mary rushed on, her face a crimson glow as she stared at the white pieces of lace hanging decorously from her fingers. They seemed frozen in the air. "Mike was kind enough to return these things that—" she continued, but Mike cut in just then.

"Say, Professor," he said, unsure what would come out of Mary's mouth next. He tried hard to keep the smile out of his voice. "How about if I stop by later to see about that door you told me was stuck—"

Mary escaped into the shadow of the doorway. Her fingers closed tightly around the underwear and she finally managed to shove it into the pocket of her robe. When she looked up Professor Atwood was strolling down the elm-shaded lane, a small smile across his lined face.

Mike was standing quietly on the step, his hands shoved into his pockets, his eyes bright and smiling. "Nice man, the professor."

Mary wiped her damp forehead with the back of her hand. "Yes, he is nice. Very proper."

"Oh, I don't know. Beneath that rather formidable exterior I bet there's quite an imagination. And right this minute it's probably working overtime on possible explanations for that." He nodded toward her pocket. "I have to admit it gave me a thought or two."

Mary leaned against the door frame. "Oh? Well, those are the pitfalls of cohabiting in a dryer, I guess."

Mike laughed. "Very lovely pitfalls, I might add."

Mary was trying to relax, but discussing her underwear with Mike simply wasn't doing the trick. "Would you like some coffee?" she asked, attempting a change in direction. "And as payment for the delivery, I'll throw in a bagel."

Mike shook his head. "Sorry, I'll have to take a rain check. I was due on the other side of campus about five minutes ago. It's a busy time of year around here."

Mary nodded and tried to hide her disappointment behind a smile. "You're right. I'd better follow your example and get myself together."

"Tomorrow is a little more open. Maybe I can show you around. Believe it or not, there're more exciting things to see around Chestershire than the Laundromat."

"Impossible—"

"Trust me," he said with a grin. "You free anytime?"

Mary thought through the next day, a Sunday and the last before classes started. There was a reception at the president's home at three, but that was it, other than finalizing her class preparations.

But there was a time and place for everything. And tomorrow she would make the time to be in the same place as Mike Gibson. "Sure," she said. "How does four sound?"

"Four sounds fine." He started to walk away, then turned back and smiled at her, that same half smile she'd seen in the Laundromat. It was an unnerving kind of smile, touched with laughter and a certain carelessness. "One more thing," he said. "Your days of sharing dryers are over, for now, anyway."

"What do you mean?"

"I checked into it this morning and the university has a couple of small washer-dryer units that aren't being used. They're going to send one over today."

"What? Just like that?"

The smile was still there, a little broader now. He snapped his fingers. "Just like that. Magic."

"But—"

"It's done. So long, Mary Shields."

And he left.

She watched him as he walked away, down the short shaded path and east toward the hub of the campus. Head back, he was looking up now at an intricate network of branches webbed overhead, or maybe beyond at the sky. He had shoved his hands into his pockets and his long, well-proportioned figure commanded the narrow pathway. There was a slight swagger to his long stride, more athletic than arrogant. Mary wondered briefly what he taught, and then realized with a start that they hadn't discussed any factual things about themselves at all. For all she knew he was a dean, or he could be a student. There were many older ones on campuses these days. No, she decided, he was a teacher. She would bet on it. And that was why he could get her a dryer with a bat of his eye. He probably knew someone who knew someone.

And then, with a small smile of anticipation at finding out more about Mike Gibson, Mary tightened her robe about her and slipped back indoors.

Chapter Two

The president's tea was held precisely at three o'clock the next afternoon. *High tea at the palace*, Mary mused, as she walked up the winding flower-bordered walk that led to the spacious colonial house in which the college president and his wife lived. The house was built on a hilly tract of land right in the center of campus. Today it was dappled with afternoon sunlight and lovely shadows spread across the deep green shutters of the house and the carefully tended flower beds. It was perfect, a movie-set kind of place.

Ahead of Mary an elderly couple walked at a leisurely pace, the woman's arm tucked securely into the man's, their heads bent together companionably. The woman wore a large straw hat with bright flowers tucked into the yellow band. Farther ahead was a group of younger faculty. A tall sandy-haired man stood head-and-shoulders above the three women gathered around him. Mary's gaze lingered on the back of his head.

Mike Gibson? she wondered.

She peered around the slow-moving couple, but the group had moved through the open doors and she lost sight of them. She was again surprised at the pleasurable ripple that had come and gone at the thought of Mike. It was the familiarity, she supposed. She had found Mike comfortable and easy to talk to. And she knew her hesitancy around strangers sometimes moved her that way, to the cool, safe shadow of someone else who was more outgoing. Her agent often teased her about her shy remoteness on the one hand and her clear, tough set of professional goals on the other. "You're an enigma, Mary," Henry Capra would say as he puffed on a fat cigar.

"Just a study in contrasts," Mary would answer.

Well, Mary thought, she wouldn't be shy here on this lovely peaceful Indiana campus, nor would she worry about her goals. For these weeks she'd immerse herself in teaching others to do what she loved so much, writing. Mary ran the palm of her hand down the side of her blue silk dress. Then she smiled in an appropriate reception-like way, and walked into the cool, spacious entry hall to shake the hands of her hostess and host.

The president of Chestershire College and his wife greeted her cordially, introduced her to several people standing nearby and then left Mary on her own to wander around the lovely home and veranda and meet her fellow faculty.

She looked over the sea of faces, the gracious, smiling knots of people looking like colorful flowers in a waving meadow. Her polite smile relaxed into one of pleasure.

Mary met one faculty member after another, until one name melted into the next. The conversation was soft and subdued, but riding on an undercurrent of anticipation for the opening day of classes. Mary listened to the talk with one ear, her smile holding its own and her eyes drifting from group to group, searching for a tall, handsome man who slept so soundly on Laundromat benches.

"You may miss New York for a while," a well-dressed woman several years Mary's senior said as they stood together drinking sparkling punch from small crystal cups. "I did briefly when I came onto the music faculty here. I missed the crises and the noise."

Mary laughed. "I've noticed there's not much of either of those here. For several days it was so quiet I couldn't sleep."

"You needed a good screech of tires, no doubt, a few fender benders outside your window—"

"Yes," Mary said, with a laugh. "And some sirens thrown in for good measure." She looked over the woman's shoulder at several newcomers, then focused back in on the friendly music teacher. "Do you...do you by any chance know Mike Gibson?" The question simply slipped out of nowhere, a stray sentence tacked onto the words that came before it.

The woman accepted the question without surprise. "Mike? Oh, yes. He's a lovely man."

Mary placed her cup carefully on the white tablecloth. "I haven't seen him here this afternoon."

"Here? No, I don't suppose you have—" The woman's voice broke off, then came back with a start. "What is happening?!"

All across the room hands instinctively shot up into the air. A chorus of surprised voices filled the room. And then the fine mist registered for what it was, and dozens of heads turned upward.

From small jets crisscrossing the high textured ceiling, came a relentless spray of cold water. In seconds, it covered the flower-decorated tables, the tiny watercress sandwiches and nearly forty-five well-dressed faculty members of Chestershire College.

Mary stood and stared, first at the mist that now shrouded the room, and then at the comical antics of the surprised guests. And then she began to move, scooping up a small oriental rug and carrying pictures and books from the room. Several others did the same, and soon the room was a flurry of activity and Mary almost failed to see Mike, wouldn't have seen him, in fact, except she was spreading books out on the floor in the entry hall as he rushed in and he almost tripped over her bent figure.

"Mary, hi!" he said, pausing for a second at her side. He forked one hand through his hair as he surveyed the chaos.

She looked up from where she was crouched. "Isn't this something? You're just in time—"

"So they tell me," he said, his eyes sparkling as they met hers. "Never a dull moment around here, is there?" He brushed a band of damp hair from his forehead. "I'll see you in a minute," and then he was gone, striding across the marble hallway in long, purposeful steps.

It was not until the sprays stopped and Mike returned to her side later that Mary realized he was the one who had saved the day.

"Mike, my friend," President Carroll was saying, "what can I say? I certainly don't know what we'd have done without you. Perhaps you were right to talk me into giving you that blasted job." He clapped Mike on the back and as Mary watched the expansive movement she noticed that Mike was wearing jeans, free of paint this time, and a knit shirt with a sweatshirt pulled loosely down over it. He looked as handsome as she had remembered, but was definitely not in afternoon-tea attire.

Mike was laughing along with the distinguished college president. "Maybe now you'll take me up on my offer of a tour of your basement. There are a few shut off valves you might want to be introduced to."

The handsome man shook his head. "You know I've always hated stuff like that. I'd only forget. Maybe you could show Sheila." He looked over at his wife who was graciously passing out towels to the guests.

"I think maybe I will." Mike smiled again, then turned his full attention to Mary, something he'd wanted to do since he first spotted her hunched over the pile of damp books. "How did you like the tea, Mary? You can't say we don't go in for atmosphere here at Chestershire."

The small group that had gathered in the foyer laughed and Mary laughed, as well. Then Mike fell into polite chatter with the others and Mary had a chance to watch him. He worked and controlled and entertained the group effortlessly; he was totally at ease. And yet he stood out, and it wasn't just his casual dress among the party goers, she thought. There was something else, something unique about Mike Gibson.

President Carroll's wife, Sheila, joined them then and announced that more warm, dry towels would be arriving soon and hot tea and coffee were being served in the den. The *dry* den, she emphasized, and the group quickly disbanded, some following Mrs. Carroll and others making a departure.

"Are you staying?" Mike asked Mary.

Mary looked down at the silk dress, wrinkled and spotted now. The once bright flowers in the design were sad and lifeless and the dress clung uncomfortably to her body. "I think I'd better get out of this before I'm taken in for indecent exposure."

Mike's brows lifted in interest. "Nah," he said finally. "But you're freezing. Let's get you out of here and home to change, before you catch pneumonia."

Before she could object, Mike looped one arm around her shoulder and hurried her out the door and down the wide fan of stairs.

They laughed, as they hurried along, at the chaos, at the frantic scurryings of the distinguished faculty, at Bill Carroll's laid-back way of handling it.

A breeze lifted their joined laughter and spun it around above them. Then just as quickly it whipped back at the thin material of Mary's dress, pressing it flat and cold against her skin. She shivered and Mike felt it beneath the light press of his arm.

"You're freezing, Mary." He paused along the path and pulled the white sweatshirt with the tiny bluebird dotting the eye of Chestershire from his torso. "Here, this will warm you."

Mary gratefully pulled the sweatshirt over her head and pushed her arms into the sleeves. It slipped on easily, falling over her narrow hip bones and on down nearly to the bottom of her dress.

Mike watched with pleasure as the bluebird took up a new perch on the appealing mound of Mary's left breast. "Lucky little guy," he murmured.

"Hm-m-m?"

"The bluebird. He's in heaven."

Mary glanced down, then blushed, and picked up some speed as she continued down the path.

A young man from across the way waved at Mike as they passed in front of the library and Mike waved back.

"You know a lot of people here," Mary observed.

"Oh, you stay in a place long enough and you begin to get responses from everything—people, signposts, trees—"

"You've been here a long time?"

"It depends on how you measure time. Not that long really. But I grew up here."

"I guess you like it."

"Very much. It's home. I was away for a long time and it was good to come back."

Mary slanted her head back and looked up at him. He took in everything as he walked, the pathway, the buildings, the trees, and herself, as well. He didn't miss a thing. He must be an artist, she thought, absorbing the world for his art, as she did with her writing. "Mike," she said, "tell me something. Just who are you?"

Mike looked at her curiously for a long moment. He seemed to be giving serious thought to her question. But when he answered, there was a twinkle in his eye and his lips curved in a smile. "Who am I? Tilter of windmills, chaser of dreams, a fixer of faculty-tea floods—"

Mary nudged him lightly in the side. "You know what I mean. You know about me, where I fit in on this campus. But I don't know about you. You weren't at the faculty tea." She paused, and then continued. "As a guest, I mean."

"As a guest?" Mike looked at her to see if she were joking with him, and when he saw she was not he began to laugh, low, loose laughter that drove away the chill inside Mary and replaced it with a lovely warmth. "No, Mary," he said. "I guess I assumed you knew what I did here. But that was presumptuous of me—"

"I only thought—I mean, the sweatshirt. And President Carroll obviously knows you—"

"Sure, it's understandable. An oversight on my part." He was still smiling and he took her arm, turning her down the path that led to her cottage. "Bill Carroll and I have known each other for years. His family and mine have been friends for a long time, and Bill and I are friends. And as for the sweatshirt, they'll sell those things to anyone with twenty bucks. I work here, Mary, but I'm not teaching. Right now I fix things. I work for the maintenance department on campus."

"Maintenance?" For a moment the word held no meaning for Mary. And then it all fit into place. Maintenance, broken sprinkler systems, the paint on his jeans. And even his comment to Professor Atwood the day before. She laughed. "Oh, Mike, how dumb of me!"

"Not dumb at all. There was no reason you should have known who I was."

"But you know so many people here. I guess I just assumed—"

"Sure, I understand. My father taught here for a long time, and you're right, I do know a lot of people."

"Did you go to Chestershire yourself?"

"No. I went away to college."

"Where?"

"Harvard."

He said it quietly, matter-of-factly, as if the entire Chestershire College maintenance department probably did a stint at Harvard before getting on with their lives. Mary was about to press the issue, when Mike looked down at her and tugged at a lock of her hair. "Did you know your hair gets even curlier when it's wet?"

The topic was changed and Mary accepted the switch without a struggle. She had known Mike less than forty-eight hours and certainly had no right to pry into his life. So she concentrated on his teasing and hoped that later there'd be time to learn more about him. "This hair was the bane of my youth, Mike. I used to try and iron it to get the curls out."

"Ingenious."

"You wouldn't say that if you had seen the results."

Mike laughed. "I bet you kept your mother busy."

"My mother died when I was born."

The energetic sound of a flock of birds filled in the sudden silence and Mike walked along beside Mary, lost in thought. He was thinking about her, about this gentle-looking creature growing up without a mother. His own mother was such a force in the Gibsons' family life that he found it difficult to imagine the concept of family without a mother at the center of it.

"My father raised me," Mary said a short while later. "He was a good man, a *successful* man—"

"Was? Then your father is gone, too."

"Yes. My father died a couple of years ago. He was a busy, small-town doctor in upstate New York until his illness."

"And that's where you were raised?"

Mary nodded.

"Then you're not big-city, after all. We've something in common, Mary—two kids raised in small-town America."

"Yes, in a way. But with a major difference."

"What's that?"

"You seem to like small-town living. I'll never go back to it."

There was such conviction in her voice Mike turned to look at her. Her eyes were bright and earnest. "What happened to you there?"

"Let's say that ironing my hair was a high point. I led a very uneventful life. I think that's why I started writing—I could make up things, invent a new life with wonderful possibilities."

"And there aren't possibilities in small towns?"

"For some, maybe."

Mike paused as they reached the steps to Mary's bungalow. He turned Mary slightly so he could look more closely into her eyes.

"What?" she asked.

"Your eyes. They're not the eyes of someone who's led a quiet, uneventful life."

Mary quickly turned away and unlocked the door. "Well, they are, and I did. Quiet. Unassuming. Boring—" The last word drifted off as Mary walked on inside.

Mike followed. "And that's all in the past for you—"

"Absolutely." Mary motioned for Mike to go on into the small living room. "And buried forever."

She smiled, then, a quick, stirring smile that caused an unexpected flip somewhere inside him. Mike coughed.

Mary started down the hall, tossing back over her shoulder as she moved, "Make yourself at home, Mike. I'll be back in three shakes of a lamb's tail—as they say in small-town America."

Mike laughed and then she was gone, and in seconds he heard the rhythmic spray of the shower. He looked around the sparsely furnished living room. It was neat and clean, but without a trace of the lovely young woman whose past life seemed to evoke such strong feelings. There were no pictures, no small touches. Mike shrugged. Well, she probably had not bothered to bring a lot of stuff since she would not be here long. He thought of his own home, filled with color and reminders of all the things in his life that had brought him joy. And then he shrugged, feeling a sudden, unexpected wave of sadness. He walked briskly across the small braided rug and into the kitchen. Food. That was what he needed. He had not eaten for hours.

When Mary walked in a short while later, her hair wet and shining and a bright red jumpsuit warming her body, Mike was standing in front of the refrigerator looking disillusioned.

"This is the most godforsaken refrigerator I've ever seen," he said.

Mary walked across the room and looked over his shoulder. "How can you say that? Yogurt, Diet Coke, wheat germ—that's the stuff great novelists are nurtured on."

The clean scent of soap drifted about Mike. Mary's presence behind him was alarmingly conspicuous. "Inhuman," he said brusquely.

He paused for a minute as if trying to regain something and then he looked at Mary with the friendly sparkle back in his eye. "There's a great pub down on Fifth Street, with the fattest, juiciest, greasiest burgers in the Midwest. And there's an obnoxious but lovable waitress named Ruthie, for added flavor. Come on—you'll love it."

Mary nodded silently and smiled back at him, masking the emotion of moments before. She had felt it, too, the sudden awareness of one another, the tug inside of her that was a response to more than a friendly face in a strange town. She bit down hard on her bottom lip, then turned and followed Mike unquestioningly into the fading light of the Indiana autumn day.

Chapter Three

The next day the writers' workshop began and Mary gave her full attention to the eager students who sat around the polished round table. She thought of herself at that age, vibrant and eager to learn, but with no ready guidance such as these students had, no place to go with her ideas, no one to offer her encouragement. She would give these kids everything she herself had wanted; she would encourage and critique and cry and laugh at the words they put to paper. She would be the mentor she had never had.

And she was.

By week's end the group had melded into a vibrant whole and creative juices flowed as vigorously as the Lark River, which meandered along the edge of town. Mary was in seventh heaven.

She walked along a shadowy campus path, her books pulled up tight to her chest and her mind traveling over the week. The only dimness in the days had been not seeing Mike. He had entered into her thoughts often, this nice new friend. More than once she had had the odd sensation of wanting to share with him, of wanting to go over the bright moments in the week's workshop with him. It was odd because she had never had a close friend quite like that, not one with whom she could share her thoughts. Her diaries and books provided the intimacy she needed, and she had always preferred it that way. People had their place, certainly, but not within the privacy of her thoughts.

Mike Gibson was different, somehow, and she wanted him to know how well things had gone. But he hadn't called and she hadn't run into him, so she had pulled her thoughts to herself.

And then, as if her mind had sent a message directly to him, she heard his voice from across a small clearing on campus, from the other side of a white gazebo near her building.

"Mary," he called out, and seconds after the welcome sound of his voice reached her ears, he had strode across the grass and caught up with her.

"Hey, lovely lady," he said, "how was your week?"

Mary laughed, delighted to see him. "My week was wonderful, Mike. It really was!"

"Well, that's what I hear, as well, so it must be true." He matched his stride with hers. "I hear, and I quote, 'She's absolutely inspiring!'"

Mary laughed. "The kids are terrific. That's all it is. But I am having a wonderful time."

"So we have a convert here, and now you're all set to settle down in a small bungalow and devote yourself to nurturing the minds of youth."

"Oh, no! No, no. Not in a million years." Mary laughed, and it caught on a breeze and spun around them. "This is a wonderful break, being here for these weeks. A kind of vacation. But this isn't for me, not permanently."

"So, a week hasn't taken the big-city fever out of you?"

"Oh, it's not just the big city, Mike. It's the whole world I want. I want to see and taste every single bit of it."

Mike smiled at her enthusiasm. She seemed, at that moment, far younger than her years. She was a young woman getting her first taste of life. "Then I bet you will. And I suppose when you do, it will all be grist for the writing mill."

"That's it, exactly."

"I can understand wanting all that, I guess. I love it here, now, but everyone's different. Some people need the world. And then there are those content to spend it in the shade of an Indiana rain tree. Each to his own."

"But you know, Mike, I've been thinking about that."

"What's that?"

"You. Here. There's something that doesn't sit right—"

Mike was silent for a minute. Then he looked down at her and grinned. "Never judge a book by its cover."

"Of course not. And I don't know you well enough to make assumptions. But my intuition says there's more to Michael Gibson than meets the eye."

Mike laughed heartily. "Good. No one ever thought of me as mysterious before. I kind of like it."

"Well, now that I've expounded on my incredible week, tell me how yours went?"

"Not bad. Lots of work, and I missed a few days, which always causes major pileups."

"Oh? Were you sick?"

"No, I spent a couple of days in Indianapolis."

"Business or pleasure?"

"Neither, really. My kid brother, Andrew, is studying to be an ophthalmologist at the med center there."

"That's nice, having a brother close by. Is he your only sibling?"

"Oh no, not by a long shot. There's a bunch of us. Sam lives in D.C. He works at the Pentagon. Kate's a lawyer—"

"Impressive."

Mike shrugged. "There are no Indian chiefs as far as I know, but you get your pick of nearly everything else."

"How many of you are there?"

"Seven."

Mary gasped.

Mike laughed. "My mother would have had more, if she could have. She loves kids."

"And your father?"

"Oh, sure, he loves kids, too. He didn't like hassles, though, but as long as Mom kept the house running smoothly, and she did that with one arm tied behind her back, it was fine with him to keep the cribs filled."

"I can't imagine a family like that. There was only me and my father. Just the two of us." Mary shivered involuntarily. That life was so far away from her now, a dark shadow on her memory, but not real in a significant way. Thinking about it was uncomfortable, so she closed her eyes tight and forced the images to disappear.

"Sometimes, when I was a kid, I thought it would be nice to be an only child," Mike said.

Mary's eyes shot open. "An only child? No, you wouldn't want that, not ever." She spoke with startling conviction, and then she quickly changed the subject. "What did you study at Harvard?" she asked.

"Oh, this and that. I loved college. Business was my major, but that was academic, really."

No, Mary scolded herself. She wouldn't do it. She would not ask him why he had gone to Harvard business school to become a fix-it man!

"I liked Cambridge," Mike went on. "It was a great place, stimulating, so I ended up staying up there for grad school."

Mary bit down on her bottom lip.

They came to a small bridge that curved over a stream running through the center of campus and walked across it slowly. Mary watched Mike's profile as he talked. Maybe she could read there the answer to all her questions. But she couldn't; Mike's face was a wonderful blend of easy smiles and intelligence, but it didn't explain anything. And then she chastised herself. Maybe there was nothing to explain. Maybe Mike simply *liked* this kind of work. Maybe he was a Renaissance man, the kind of person who could save a faculty tea with a wrench and common sense, who walked across campus with the air of a man in touch with life, a . . . a Don Quixote, an artist, who just happened to have a graduate degree from Harvard's school of business administration.

"I've lost you, haven't I?" Mike asked from a distance.

Mike had crossed the bridge and was looking at her from the other side. "What? Oh, Mike, I'm sorry. I crawled inside my head for a minute." She hurried across the bridge after him.

"I'd give more than a penny for what just went on in there," he said.

"Nope. What's in there is all mine."

"Doesn't it come out in your writing? I thought that's what writers did, sift through experiences and then write about them."

"Yes, but only after there's been time to disguise it all."

"I'll have to remember that."

"I couldn't write about you, Mike. Not yet, anyway."

"Oh?"

"I need to understand someone, at least to catch a glimpse of his soul, before I can write about him."

"Aha. Plumb the depths and all that."

He laughed again and Mary watched the tiny lines fan out from his electric blue eyes. She wondered briefly if she could capture a face such as Mike's in words, or whether only an artist could do it justice.

Beside her, Mike went on talking. "I think you might be disappointed if you plumbed my depths, Mary. I'm pretty simple."

"The best depths to plumb. Simple is sometimes the most riveting."

A dimple flashed as he listened to her, and Mary was momentarily distracted by it. He watched her carefully as she talked, as if he were listening with his eyes as well as his ears.

In a short time, which passed too quickly for Mary, they were at the small walkway that led to her cottage.

Mike feigned a small bow. "Here you are ma'am, one writer delivered safe and sound."

Mary glanced at the small home. "How did we get here so fast?"

"Magic."

"I guess. Well, thanks, Mike. I enjoyed the company." Mary searched her mind for something else to say. She did not want him to leave. She did not want the easy conversation to stop.

"I'm happy your week went well, Mary," he said.

"Thank you."

"I think we need to mark it somehow, acknowledge it, don't you?"

Her eyes lifted.

"Any plans for tonight?"

"None, whatsoever."

"Good. You do now."

He grinned and then left, after telling her to dress comfortably, to bring a sweater, and to not stuff on wheat germ because dinner would be incredible.

Mike picked her up two hours later in a red pickup truck, his jeans fresh, his slightly long hair still damp from the shower. A lump formed in Mary's throat as she watched him walk up the brick walkway. She had the disarming feeling that she had known Mike for a long, long time, perhaps a lifetime. It was an awareness that she found overwhelming.

"Hi," Mike said when he reached the door. "Ready? Here, this is for you." He handed her a small, clumsily wrapped package.

"Mike..."

"It's a remembrance of your first week of teaching. Go ahead, open it."

Mary blushed, then eagerly tore off the silver wrapping. She lifted out a small, thin book. The pages were yellowed with age and the pebbled leather cover had a single title in faded gold leaf: *A Writer's Meanderings*.

Mary stared at it, running her fingers over the worn leather. The lump in her throat grew until it hurt.

"It seemed appropriate," Mike was saying beside her.

"Oh, Mike—" She looked up at him finally.

"Hey, I'm sorry if you think it's out of line—"

Mary closed her eyes briefly and shook her head. "No, no Mike. I'm touched, that's all. I'm not used to presents, and this is so...so thoughtful. It's...it's perfect."

"I'm glad. You worried me for a minute there. Now let's get going. If we don't get to food soon, I may disintegrate."

Mary's full attention was still on the book. "Where did you get this, Mike? It's a first edition. It's valu—"

"Used bookstore in California a long time ago," he said without letting her finish. "I love old books. Now come on, Mary, because if that book is going to detain eating any longer, I'm going to take it back."

Mary hugged it to her chest. "No, you're not. Not ever." She set it down carefully on the table inside the door, grabbed a sweater and followed Mike out to the truck.

"Where are we going?" she asked. They were driving down Third Street toward the edge of town.

"A wonderful place. You'll love it. It's not far."

"I must be hungrier than I thought. I can almost smell food."

Mike smiled and they lapsed into a comfortable silence. Mary concentrated on the rolling Indiana countryside passing them by. Thick woods hugged the narrow highway and the trees shimmered in the setting sun.

"It's so pretty here."

"This isn't anything compared to what it will be in a few weeks when the leaves turn. We'll come back this way then and you'll see real beauty. It's an artist's paradise."

"We'll come back," Mary repeated in her head. *You and me*, as naturally as if they had grown up next door to one another. The words were nice, comforting. Mary settled back and wondered at the irony of it all. She had come all this way, nearly half a country—and she had found a friend.

After a while the trees fell away and a small town with cobblestone streets rose up out of the countryside. Mike slowed and they drove down the main street. It was lined with dozens of small shops.

"This is Nashville, Indiana," Mike said. "It happens to be home of the best fried biscuits in the world."

"We're eating here?"

"No, this is the place we get biscuits." He pulled up to the curb before an old building. There was a sign out front that read *Nashville House,* and Mary followed him through a small courtyard and on inside. They were in a room that resembled an old country store, stuffed with knickknacks, boxes of candy and small key chains that said *Nashville* on them.

"The restaurant is through there," Mike said, pointing over the tops of jars of marmalade and honey. They squeezed through the aisles and moved through another door where a round-cheeked waitress stood at the reservation podium and greeted Mike with a huge smile. "Awl ready for ya, Mike," she said. She handed him a fragrant white sack and a small jar of apple butter, then asked him about his family.

Mary listened to their friendly chatter with half an ear. Mike seemed to have friends everywhere.

Mike stopped on the way out and bought her a kitchen witch to hang above the window in her bun-

galow—"It'll ward off evil kitchen spirits" he told her,
"and make sure your bagels don't burn."

And then they were off again, driving on through the
small town.

A short distance later, Mike pulled off the main
highway onto a narrow winding road that threaded
through thick woods. He drove a quarter of a mile,
then pulled off into a small clearing. "All right, at last!
Here we are, milady. A celebratory meal to beat 'em
all."

Mary looked straight ahead. The truck was parked
on a patch of gravel bordered by a split-rail fence. A
short distance ahead, its shoreline outlined by hundreds of pine trees, spruce trees and old oak trees, was
a gentle lake. Mary stared.

"You like it? You can't beat the view, and it seemed
more special than sitting in a noisy restaurant." He was
out of the truck's cab before Mary could answer and
began pulling brown sacks from the back.

"You're something else, you know that, Mike Gibson?" she called around to the rear of the truck. "Has
anyone ever told you you have a romantic streak?"

"Not for a while. Come on, grab a bag."

Mary followed him along the short path to a soli-
tary picnic table that sat beside a stone barbecue pit.
The only sound in the air was the soft crunch of pine
needles beneath their feet as they walked along the
spongy path and the slight rustle of woodland animals
scurrying for cover. Mary sighed. "I think I'm in
heaven."

"Close. This is Lake Manitou. I think it's the next best thing." He put his armload of bags down on the table. "Now, the downside of this operation is there are no waitresses."

"Definitely not a downside," Mary said.

"Good. My thoughts exactly. But it means you'll have to work. And your first job is to find some dry twigs so we can get this thing started." Mike motioned toward the grill. "Why don't you check that trail over there."

Mary grinned, saluted and was off. When she returned a short time later, the table was set with a white cloth and small candles. Flames flickered in the light breeze and the heavy crystal holders held down the table covering. Tall, slender wineglasses and two place settings completed the elegant picnic site. Mike was nearby, eyeing the bottle of champagne he had taken from the cooler.

"I know someone in New York who writes romance novels," Mary said. "I think she needs to talk with you."

Mike looked over at the table. "You like it?"

"Of course, I like it. This is wonderful."

"I thought your first week of teaching needed a special celebration."

Mary stuck the dry twigs into the grill and stepped back while Mike ignited them. "This is...this is an awfully nice thing for you to do, Mike."

"I think you're not used to people being nice to you."

"I don't know. I think I just don't make time for this kind of thing often."

"No time to have picnics in New York?"

Mary laughed. "Okay, rain tree man, score one for Indiana."

Mike poured two glasses of champagne and handed her one. "I'm not trying to convince you of anything, honest. I left here for a long time myself. It isn't that I think it's the only place to live."

The cool champagne bubbled down her throat while she listened to him. "Where did you live?"

"I worked in glorious California for a while. How about you—is New York your one and only state?"

Mary nodded. "And until three years ago it was only upstate New York. I didn't even go away to college."

"You were a homebody, I guess."

Mary settled herself beneath a fat oak tree under which Mike had spread a thick plaid blanket. "Yes, I was a homebody, but not by choice."

"I suppose it was important to your father to have you there."

"It was important to him, yes." Mary sipped her champagne slowly, her eyes focused out on the lake. Mike sat down next to her. As he watched her, it occurred to him that there was something profoundly sad about the lovely Mary Shields. The whimsy that he had felt in her before was completely missing now, and her eyes held a faraway look.

"I think I've brought up something that makes you sad."

"No. Well, yes, but it's okay. My years in Pine-wood Falls were kind of lonely as a kid. My dad was always so busy."

"He never remarried?"

"It wasn't for lack of opportunity. My father was the most eligible widower in Murdoch County. Every-body loved Dad. There were women coming by all the time, nurses from the hospital, ladies from the church. Our house was always filled with cakes and pies and freshly made loaves of bread."

Mike laughed. "Sounds terrific."

"No, no, it wasn't," Mary said with unusual inten-sity. "I was a blimp. I ate my way through every one of those pies and cakes."

Mike eyed her slender body. "You'd have fooled me."

"*Years* of discipline and pain!"

Mike laughed. "And your father? What did he think of all these ladies?"

"I don't think he was even aware of all the women who went in and out, fixing us dinner, mending clothes, cleaning the house. One of them, Haddie Sheehan, was our housekeeper, and he noticed her sometimes, but not significantly. He never had time."

"He worked hard?"

"An understatement. My dad was the savior of the entire county and he took his reputation very seri-ously. He would go out and see patients at two in the morning or eleven at night. He was incredible. He al-ways kept a fresh shirt in his car and some in his office, too, because sometimes he didn't make it home for days. He loved his work. He loved his patients."

Mike watched the mixture of emotions that passed across Mary's face. There was such intensity there that it was nearly painful to watch. And then she smiled, that soft, perfect smile that sent his concern scattering. "He was a *good* doctor. The very best."

"I'm sure he was."

"And when he suddenly became ill, it was awful for him. You know how it would be, someone who had always been vital, involved, to have to curtail everything that had been meaningful in his life—" Mary stopped. She shivered. Mike was doing it again, watching her so carefully, listening so intently, and it was her soul she was spewing out this time.

"Go on, Mary," he urged, leaning slightly toward her.

Mary took a gulp of her champagne. It slid down easily now, all the way down to her stomach, soothing, smoothing out the knots that had begun to grow there. "That's all I was going to say. He had a hard time once he became ill—"

"Sure, I can imagine. Especially since he didn't have time to prepare for it."

"Yes, that's right."

Her voice was softer now, and Mike noticed she spoke more carefully. "Did he go to a nursing home?" he asked.

"No. He stayed home. The ladies continued to bring their cakes and pies and stews, so that was a help, and I was there to care for him."

"How long was he sick?"

"All in all, it was about eight years."

Mike swallowed hard. He spoke the words solemnly, carefully. "And you cared for him all that time?"

"In the beginning he could still work some. And we had nurses at the end. But he wanted me. He wouldn't let anyone else do certain things for him. It had to be me."

Eight years. She had devoted eight years to caring for her father. No wonder she wanted to see the world. She was a bird set free, finally, after years in a cage.

"May I have another glass of champagne?" Mary asked. "This is wonderful. And enough talk about things past. The present is far too delicious to waste on all that."

Mike poured her wine silently, thinking about what she had said. Mary was talking about herself in a way he could tell did not come easily. But even at that, Mike was sure there were many emotions bottled up inside Mary Shields that had never seen the light of day. He got up and put two steaks on the grill. The sizzle of fat on hot coals scattered the silence and the aroma of charcoal and steak filled the air.

"It smells wonderful." Mary was standing just behind him, her chin nearly touching his back.

"It *is* delicious. I'm a hell of a cook. I thought I told you that before."

She nodded. "Right. I forgot. Now about those biscuits..." Mary pulled open the white sack and peered inside.

"Okay, okay. One, though, and that's all till dinner."

Mary pulled out two round tan biscuits, each the size of a fat Ping-Pong ball, and bit into one. She closed her eyes and swallowed. "Well?"

Mary opened her eyes. "Wonderful."

"I told you." He took the other from her fingers and swallowed it in a few bites. "This is the best spot in the world. And you can't come here without biscuits. It's kind of a Hoosier law." He speared each steak and turned it over. "When I was in California my mom used to pack up these biscuits and send them to me. You get addicted—"

A streak of fading sunlight fell through the trees and across Mike's face, painting interesting shadows and highlighting the angle of his cheekbones. Mary watched, fascinated. She couldn't move her eyes from his face. No, she thought, the biscuits were great, but food wasn't the compelling thing here, nor the addiction. There was something else going on. It was a feeling, a happy, joyous kind of feeling that filled her as she stood here beside Mike Gibson. It was the way watching him moved her insides around. That's what could become an addiction...

"Are all writers like you?"

Mary focused on the voice. "Wh-what?"

"You slip into your mind as easily as a duck into water. And then I've lost you and I haven't any idea where you've gone."

Mary laughed. "You're trying to say, in a very nice way, that I'm spacy. Or moody. I like to think of it as my creative mode. I kind of take what's going on around me and suck it in, assimilate it and then come back out for more when I'm ready."

"Interesting process," Mike mused. He turned slightly away from her and fiddled with the steaks. Damn, whatever made him bring her out here? She'd gotten him all stirred up. It was that voice, throaty and quiet, and packed full of vulnerability. It was also sexy, sexy as hell.

"Mike?"

"Yeah."

"You keep staring at the steaks. I think they're done."

"Sure," he said gruffly, his eyes focusing on the meat. "I was just going to take them off."

Mary watched him and took a step backward.

They were involved in some sort of dance here and she wasn't sure, at all, that she knew all the steps. A breeze ruffled her hair and cooled the back of her neck. Good, that's what she needed, a little cooling off. It was probably a result of the euphoria of her first week's teaching. She and Mike were friends, odd, mismatched friends, at best, and that was it. They were an interlude in one another's lives, that was all. And there was absolutely no sense in letting hormones mess up a lovely friendship.

She looked up at Mike. "Food. We need food."

"Lots of food," Mike agreed. "And more champagne. *Cold* champagne."

They ate their elegant picnic dinner while a scattering of ducks in the middle of the lake performed for them, dipping beneath the water, then skimming its surface with barely a ripple trailing behind. While they watched, the sun began to sink down in slow motion into the still waters, leaving the sky a blended kaleidoscope of reds and yellows and purple-colored bands. A pine-scented breeze rustled the trees, and Mary and Mike ate until there was nothing left but brown flakes of biscuits and nearly bare T-bones on their plates.

"There's still some champagne left," Mike said as they put the plates and glasses into a sack. "Let's welcome the night with it."

Mary smiled happily. The night, the wonderful meal and the happy exhaustion of the week all settled inside her like down filling and she followed Mike down to the edge of the water, feeling as weightless as the evening breeze. They sat together on a small wooden bench beneath a tree.

"To the night," Mike said, clinking her glass against the rim of his own.

"To *our* night," Mary added.

"And to us."

"And our friendship."

They sipped the champagne slowly. Mary's shoulder touched Mike's and she leaned lightly into it. And in front of them, as breathlessly beautiful as a Monet painting, twilight faded into the velvety darkness of night.

"There it is," Mary said, at last, pointing with her wineglass to the first star in the sky.

"Time to wish." He wrapped one arm around her shoulder. "I wish I may, I wish I might—"

"Sh-h-h," Mary said, her eyes sparkling as bright as the star. "Say it silently, and it will more surely come true." She shut her eyes.

Mike watched the moonlight warm her face. The stirring came back, but he allowed its pleasure now. "I wonder what a writer wishes for," he mused aloud. "A Pulitzer Prize? National Book Award?"

Mary shook her head. Her hair brushed lightly against his cheek. "None of those things, Mike. Those are things you work for. A writer wishes for the same things as a painter, a handyman—" She looked up into his eyes. "A writer wishes for happiness...and for lasting friendships."

Their eyes locked. Mary felt her heart beating against the wall of her chest. She wondered if Mike felt it, too.

"And a handyman, well versed in tight joints and all that, seals those wishes so they can't get away," Mike said. His voice was tight, the words coming in stops and starts. And then he kissed her, gently and deeply, with all the emotion that had been building up in him all night. Her lips were soft and lovely and perfect.

Finally Mary pulled away. She took a deep breath and then looked out over the dark surface of the lake.

Mike was silent.

Finally Mary said, "Say something, Mike."

"I like kissing you."

"That's not what I meant—"

"You like kissing me?"

"We're short-term friends, one semester..."

"I know." His voice was husky. "I shouldn't have done that, that's what you're wanting me to say. But I enjoyed it too much to say that. Besides, it would be a bold-faced lie."

Mary smiled. "I...I agree, but—"

"So let's just let it be, Mary. A sort of friendship rite..."

"A friendship rite?"

"Yeah, you know, like kids do to be blood brothers—" His head was bending low again, closer to hers, but Mary did not move. She looked up into the bottomless darkness of his eyes, and a small, throaty sigh escaped between her lips.

"That's what I say, too," Mike said, just a second before making sure they had done the kiss correctly.

Chapter Four

Mary flew into the building. Her hair was wild, her heart soaring. She had never, not in a million years, expected this. And yet it had happened, or at least was going to. And to her. While she was in Chestershire, of all the crazy places. She would have to leave New York more often.

"Is Mike Gibson around?"

An older woman sitting at a desk looked up. "Mike? He left a short while ago."

"Do you know where he went?" Mary caught her breath.

"Home, I believe. It's after five."

"Home," Mary repeated. *Home...where was that?* She'd seen Mike almost every day these past couple weeks, for a cup of coffee, a Coke, or to walk across the campus together. But she didn't know where the place was he called home. It was much easier being friends on campus, Mary had decided. Neither mentioned their friendship rite, and it was only in her private thoughts that she acknowledged the pleasure it had brought to her. She knew Mike was being nice, romantic, chivalrous, moved by the moment, but she also knew it didn't mean anything.

One day they had met at the student union and Mike had brought her here, to this small building wedged in between the art building and Carmichael's, a crowded café where the students hung out. "My office," he had said, with laughter in his eyes, and then he had led her down a flight of stairs and into a workshop. After Mary had admired the tools of his trade, the cables and electrical pieces and hammers and saws, he had treated her to one of Gibson's heroes, the sandwich they had shared in the Laundromat that very first day they'd met. He had invited her to come back to his office anytime, and if he was out, he said, Ruth, the office manager, would know where he was.

So she'd come back today to share her incredible news with her good friend. "Do you—" Mary started, and then she paused.

"Do I know where Mike lives?" Ruth finished. "Sure do."

And then without hesitation she gave Mary the instructions, telling her to keep her eyes peeled for the Dew Drop Inn sign, because that was where you turned off to find Mike's place.

Mary rushed home to her cottage and devoured a sandwich, then changed to slacks and set out. Mike had loaned her his bike so she could get around campus and she used it now, heading south toward the edge of town, trying to avoid the traffic while she searched the roadside for the Dew Drop Inn.

She found the road easily, almost as if she knew where she were going. And yet Mike had never talked to her about his home. It had simply not come up. One night the week before, when he had given her a ride to the grocery store, they had driven through an old section of Chestershire and Mike had pointed out the house in which he had been raised and where his mother and father, now retired, still lived. It was a charming, well-kept two-story house on a shady street that was lined with other equally lovely homes, spacious and homey. The yard was wide and deep, and the house appeared welcoming, the kind in which you could raise a half dozen kids comfortably. Mary had been impressed and surprised by it. She had imagined Mike's childhood to have been spent in a more rustic, understated place.

Now she turned her bike onto the gravel road that curved along behind the billboard advertising the inn. It was a hilly, ribboned road, hugged on both sides by sweet-smelling yew bushes and pines, red buds and low-growing brush. Small mailboxes marked the drives of homes on either side, but the houses themselves were secreted away, tucked back into the privacy of the woods. Mary smiled, and guided the bike carefully along the bumpy drive. This was more like it. Here she could imagine Mike living. It would be a small cabin with maybe a workshed out behind.

But when she spotted the name *Gibson* on a black metal box and turned her bike into the drive, she was in for yet another surprise. She rode her bike a few yards before she spotted his house, and then her eyes opened wide. It went beyond any kind of imagining. It seemed to grow right up out of the forest, an incredible angled redwood home that was hung with decks and skylights. From where she was, the home seemed to extend out over the side of the hill without support. A towering pine grew right up through one of the decks as the house accommodated itself to nature, bending around the forest and letting it peek through. It was magnificent, a house of light and wood, and totally at one with the environment.

And then the second surprise occurred. As Mary pedaled more quickly, anxious to get a closer look at the house, the bright blue mountain bike hit a rut in the gravel road. In the blink of an eye, before she could brake or call out, the bike careened off the side of the drive, hit a thick, fat root and sent Mary rolling down a wooded ravine.

She landed at the bottom, her head pressed into a bed of pine needles. Around her, the world spun crazily. She felt like a thrown-away rag doll. With difficulty, Mary forced herself to focus on her surroundings. Above her was Mike's bike—twisted like a pretzel around a slender birch tree. Its bright red reflector light blinked at her in the fading sunlight.

She closed her eyes and it was then she felt the throbbing in her ankle and the tiny pinpricks of discomfort from sticks and twigs and stones that were fastened brutally to her skin. She moaned softly.

A voice, familiar and foreign at the same time, rolled down the hill.

"What the . . . damn!" it said.

The sound was coming from above her, and it was deep and agitated. And then she heard the snapping of twigs beneath heavy boots and the voice came closer.

"My God, Mary, are you okay?"

It was directly above her now. She opened her eyes slowly and tried to smile. "Hi, Mike."

He crouched down on one knee. His palm rested gently on her forehead. "Are you okay?"

"My pride is shot to hell, but otherwise I guess I'm okay." She tried to lift herself up on one elbow as she was talking. Nothing moved. Her eyes opened wide. "Mike, oh, Lord, help me!"

"It's okay." He reached over and loosened her sweater from the thick tangle of bushes. "There, can you move now?"

Mary shifted, then sighed. "I thought I was paralyzed."

He shook his head. He didn't smile, his face an unnatural mask of worry and anger. "No, you were caught, that's all, but you're damn lucky. Can you move everything?"

"Everything but your bike. It's not looking terrific, Mike."

"That's the least of my worries. We'll give it some TLC."

"How about me?" She wanted him to smile, to see the light and laughter in his eyes, but Mike remained grim.

"You're sure you're okay?" he said.

"I will be, once I get out of here. Could we start by getting me up?"

Mike half smiled, then, and Mary breathed easier. She had felt somehow like an errant child. "I don't know how they do it," she said.

"Who?"

"Those monks. Or whoever it is who sleep on dry straw. It's very uncomfortable down here. I'd really like to get up now. What do you think?"

"I don't know. Maybe I should leave you here. This was a damn foolish thing to do."

"You're absolutely right." Mary lifted one hand. "Okay, I won't do it again, I promise, on my honor."

"I mean riding your bike on that loose gravel, not watching where you were going. That's what I mean."

"How do you know I wasn't watching where I was going? How do you know someone didn't throw me down here? How do you know an animal didn't run across my path, and in a heroic effort to save it, I threw myself into the ravine?"

"Because I was up in the loft and I saw you. You looked like a country kid who came into the city for the first time. What the hell were you looking at? You could have killed yourself."

"Mike, I appreciate your concern, but I want to get out of here. Then I'll give you the psychological motivation for this tumble. Okay?"

Mike, still frowning at her, put one arm around her waist and lifted her gently to her feet.

Mary winced.

"Your foot?"

She nodded. "It hurts."

"Here, put your arm around my neck."

Mary did as she was told.

Gingerly, with enormous patience, Mike helped her up the hill and across the drive to his house. By the time they reached his front door, Mike was practically carrying her, but he showed no signs of exertion.

Mary began to relax, her head lazing forward and resting on his shoulder. She steadied herself with a deep breath and it brought to her senses the clean, strong odor of the man who was helping her.

One of Mike's hands was on her waist, his fingers splayed, as he shifted her weight away from her foot. He wore a thin T-shirt today and she could feel the strength of his muscles beneath it. In fact, she could feel a great deal of Michael Gibson, far more than she wanted to pay attention to, but her imagination ignored her warnings and soared loftily. Her heartbeat quickened and images of Mike chopping wood and flinging huge logs onto a pile flashed through her mind. She could see his solid, bare chest glistening with sweat, muscles rolling beneath the sheen.

Oh, Lord, now she was hallucinating! This was ridiculous. The fall must have set off some sort of feverish reaction that was causing her to lose common sense.

"You okay?" Mike looked down at her.

"Yes," she said softly.

"You look kinda funny." He smiled at her and Mary told herself it was the smile of a brother, a guardian angel, a . . . a woodcutter. . . .

Mike pushed open the wide door and in minutes had Mary settled on a large, plump sofa in a warm high-ceiling room. He pulled up an ottoman and carefully lifted her ankle onto it. His fingers heated the delicate skin, but Mary found herself shivering.

"You're cold," he said, noticing the slight movement.

"No. Just a nervous reaction." She forced a bright smile. "You're awfully good at this," she said.

"I fix things, remember?"

"I remember." She smiled weakly.

"It hurts, doesn't it?"

It did, but the pain seemed almost a relief from the other emotions that had swept through her with unnerving velocity. Then she winced slightly as Mike gently probed the skin around her ankle bone.

"Sorry." He straightened up and walked over to a rosewood cabinet and poured some liquor into a short glass, then brought it to Mary. "Drink this, it will help."

Mary gulped down the whiskey. She coughed.

Mike smiled. "Sorry, you're not used to the hard stuff. Just sip it, Mary." He sat on the edge of the ottoman, careful not to touch her foot, and began to check her face and arms for deep scratches. "I think everything else is surface," he said after a few minutes of gentle scrutiny. "And that ankle will be better soon. It's a bad bruise, that's all. Just keep your weight off it when you can." He moved to the chair opposite her. "Now that I'm sure you'll live, would you tell me what this is all about?"

"About? Oh! I nearly forgot!" Mary shot forward in the chair, then sank back into the cushions as the pain traveled along the synapses with lightning speed. "I'm here to share my good news with you," she said, more slowly now. "I didn't know who else to tell."

"I'm a great recipient of good news. Shoot." He leaned forward, his elbows on his knees, and his open, handsome face smiling at her.

She took another quick drink of the whiskey, made a face as it went down, and began to explain. "I, me...Mary Shields...no, not me, my book, *Gideon's Gambit,* has won an award. A *terrific* award. The New York Fiction Award. Oh, Mike, it's a dream, can you believe it? Me, Mike!"

"Mary, that's...that's fantastic!"

Mary laughed. "You don't know what I'm talking about, do you?"

Mike looked at her. He laughed. "Nope. But I'm happy for you, anyway."

"The NYFA award is given by *Profiles* literary magazine. It's what everyone in the business reads, and they give three awards each year. Me...this is crazy.... Oh, Mike, it will help my career, help me be someone...."

"I think you're already someone." Mike smiled.

Mary's lashes swept her cheeks and then she looked up at Mike again. "You're very nice, but I'm not nearly what or who I want to be. I have a lot of work to do before that happens. But anyway, I was so excited when my agent called about this that I went looking for you. I needed to tell someone who would be happy with me. That's what brought me here. I wouldn't have barged in on you otherwise. I...I guess I should have called."

"It would have been less painful for you. But this is much nicer for me, and I am happy for you. What happens next with this? Will there be a ceremony?"

"Yes, a dinner."

"You'll go to New York?"

"I guess. I don't know when exactly—probably not for a few weeks. That part doesn't matter as much. But getting this affirmation matters more than I can explain."

"I can see that. I think it's great, Mary, and I have a feeling it's the first of many. Congratulations."

"Thank you." Mary rested her head back against the cushions. And then she smiled and looked around the room. "When I came out here to tell you, I thought I was coming to a little bungalow, like the one I live in.

Something modest, suitable to a man who works for Chestershire College. I don't know why, but that's what I've pictured you in. And then I turned in your drive—"

"And the rest was all downhill."

Mary grinned. She loved the laughter that fanned out from his eyes. It warmed her far more than the whiskey. "Mike, this place is absolutely breathtaking."

"You like it?"

"Like it? It's magnificent. It's not just a house in the woods, it's a woods in the house."

"Good. That's what I wanted. I planned it pretty much myself. I have a place in California, on the ocean, that has the same feeling, but this is my dream house."

"Well you should be an architect, not a handyman." Her eyes roamed around the room. It was spacious and pine-scented, with a high ceiling graced with deep skylights. One whole wall was glass, and the forest was just beyond it. Oversized chairs and couches with plump cushions of vivid Indian designs were grouped around a limestone fireplace, and warm, lovely original paintings hung on the walls. Mary wanted to curl up and never leave.

"Mike, I love it. It's such a . . . a refuge. A beautiful, lovely refuge."

Mike smiled at her effusiveness. He loved this place, and not a whole lot of people had even seen it. Oh, his good friends, of course—the Tollivers, and the rest of the small group from the college he had known long before he came back here. And his family. But not too many others. He found himself a little surprised at the pleasure of sharing it with her.

"Did you do some of the work yourself?"

"A little, but mostly I supervised and drove the guys crazy."

"It looks like a house you intend to stay in forever."

"I do."

"Mike..." Mary paused.

"No, I won't miss big cities."

Mary laughed. "No, I was going to ask you something personal, and I probably don't have any right to do it, so I stopped."

"Of course you have a right. Ask away. I won't answer if I don't want to."

Mary took a swallow of the amber liquor. "Okay," she said. "A man like you...well, I would have thought you'd be married...."

Mike laughed. "'A man like me'...I'm not sure how to interpret that, Mary."

"You're very handsome, Mike. And you're... you're..." Mary stumbled.

Mike didn't help her out. He sat back, folded his hands behind his head, and listened with a smile on his face that caused Mary to take another drink. A flush crept up her neck. She frowned, then looked at him sternly. "Okay. Face it, Gibson. You're sexy. Very sexy, in fact, in an offbeat sort of way, of course. And you have this wonderful place. I mean, I'm sure *plenty* of women would be more than happy to share it with you."

Mike was laughing openly now, his eyes sparkling with humor. "I'm making this hard on you, aren't I?"

"Damn right you are!"

"Okay. If it'll make you feel better, I *was* married once."

"Oh." The news startled her, and yet it would have been more surprising if he had not been. Of course he would have been married, she scolded herself. But it did not necessarily make her feel better.

"I was married to a nice lady," Mike went on. "We're still friends."

"But not married."

"Nope. Completely unmarried. It didn't work out."

"Does she work at the college, too?"

"Oh, no." Mike laughed. "She's like you, Mary. She loves big cities. She lives in San Francisco—that's where she's from—and she has a career there. She would never be happy here."

"So that's why you lived in California."

"Yes and no. I worked there for a while before I met her."

"You worked there? Were you . . . were you in maintenance work there?" She blushed. Damn. Mary lifted her palm to her cheek. Why should she feel awkward about his job? He loved being a handyman. He had made that perfectly clear to her. But it was confusing to her that a handyman could live in the kind of wealth implied by Mike's house. In fact, there were plenty of things about Mike Gibson that didn't fit together in an orderly way. And if he had lived in San Francisco, what was he doing in Indiana living in the woods?

"No, I did other things there," Mike was saying, and Mary tried to pull her thoughts back to the question she had asked. But Mike had already decided to change the subject. He got up and walked over to a wooden cabinet that contained the stereo. "How about some ankle-soothing music?"

Mary smiled. "Mike, you have an absolutely charming way of not answering questions."

"Thank you," he said, and she saw the flash of the dimple in his left cheek. He flicked some switches and in seconds strains of piano jazz filled the room.

"Nice," she nodded.

"Dave Brubeck."

"You like jazz?"

He nodded, then looked over at a baby grand piano on the other side of the room. It was beneath a curved wooden staircase that rose gracefully to the second level. "I'm learning to play."

Mary looked at the piano wistfully. "I took lessons for many years."

"That's great. Maybe you'll give me some pointers. A friend from the college was teaching me, but she took a sabbatical and I've been trying to plug away on my own until she comes back. I haven't had much luck, I'm afraid."

"You do so many things, Mike. You're learning the piano, you chop wood, you—"

"Chop wood?"

Mary stopped. "Did I say that?"

"Yeah."

"Oh. Well, do you?"

"Chop wood?"

Mary nodded.

"Sometimes. Strange as it may sound, no one has ever asked me about it before." He smiled at her in an unnerving way. Mary shifted in the seat. The man was reading her thoughts, she knew it. He was diving right into them, invading her private turf.

"We could make an exchange here," Mike said. "I'll teach you how to chop wood and you can teach me piano."

"Why do you want to play the piano?"

"I like music. And if I play it myself, then I don't need to depend on others to provide it for me."

"So if you end up on a desert island, you don't have to depend on a stereo—"

"Right, provided I have my piano with me," Mike said.

Mary fell easily into his laughter and accepted the wine Mike offered her in place of the harsh whiskey. She was beginning to relax, and when Mike leaned over and carefully wedged a soft pillow beneath her foot, she didn't object. His cool fingers felt good against her hot skin and the pain in her ankle began to subside to a dull throb. If she had to tumble down a hill, she had picked a good place to do it. Being here in this wonderful home, being cared for by Mike, wasn't bad at all.

No one had cared for Mary in a long time, and even then it had usually been a housekeeper whose ministrations were efficient and detached. At that moment, with the setting sun lighting his form as he leaned forward and his day-old beard shadowing the strong lines of his face, there was absolutely nothing about her handyman that seemed detached.

"Are you feeling a little better?" Mike was asking now.

Mary nodded. "Much better." She smiled.

"Good. Then I think I'll go out and check the bike for a minute." He refilled her glass with wine first, then brought a box of crackers, a hunk of cheese and set them on the small coffee table within her reach. "Okay. There. If you need anything, yell real loud and I'll probably hear you. If not, I'll be back in a few minutes." He squeezed her shoulder lightly, a casual gesture that felt oddly intimate. Mary watched him leave, then sipped her wine slowly, relieved to be alone for a few minutes. It gave her a chance to collect her thoughts, as well as to look around the room and find some answers to the question that was Mike Gibson.

She sipped her wine and let her eyes explore the lovely, softly lit room. It was the most comfortable room she had ever been in. One wall was filled with bookshelves and from where she sat Mary could see dozens of framed photographs and hundreds of books. There were current works of fiction, philosophy, art and music books. One section was filled with mostly dark-covered books and Mary noticed they were primarily business and computer books with titles that were incomprehensible to her. There were several medical books and below them a large collection of very old volumes of literature with beautiful leather covers and gilt lettering along the spine. But nowhere, as hard as she looked, could she find the kind of library she had expected. There were no fix-it books in sight. No home maintenance, no carpentry books, no plumbing books. She frowned.

And then a sudden thought struck her. Mike Gibson was a fraud. A sexy, kind, gentle, irresistible fraud. He had to be, because none of this fit, this expensive home, his degree from Harvard. No, it didn't fit at all. He could be a bookie, a janitor, a brilliant scientist. He could be . . . he could be a dangerous man, a . . .

"It's salvageable," a voice behind her said.

Mary jumped, then groaned as the pain throbbed through her ankle.

Mike was at her side in seconds. "Hey, what's wrong?"

Mary pressed her palms against her flushed cheeks. "You scared me, that's all," she said in a small voice. Damn. It was a writer's handicap, being swallowed up so completely in wild imaginings that the intrusion of reality was jarring.

"I scared you? Were you expecting someone else?"

"No, it's just that—"

Mike looked at her strangely. "What's wrong? You look like you've seen a ghost."

Mary shook her head, then took a quick gulp of wine. "No, nothing. No ghost."

"Good. I've nothing against ghosts, but I'd like them to call ahead."

"The bike's okay?" she asked, wanting desperately to move the attention from the blush that crept up her throat and onto her face.

"Not exactly okay," Mike said, "but it will be. The frame needs a good chiropractor, that's all. I'll take care of it and you can use my car, if you need it, in the meantime."

"No, I can't Mike. I can't use your car. Listen, you've already done too much for me."

"I don't need it, I have the truck: And you're not going to want to do a lot of walking."

"Let me think about it." She stared down at her foot. It was significantly swollen. "I've made a mess of your day, haven't I, dropping in like this."

"I take my drop-ins very seriously," Mike said lightly.

"You probably have plans. I'll leave."

"Plans can be changed. Would you like something to eat?"

"I ate a while ago, long before I set out to ruin your evening."

He grinned. "Good. Because there's not much here except for what you see in front of you. I need to get to the market."

He picked up the wine bottle and refilled her glass. "At least I can quench your thirst."

Mary took a long swallow. The wine had a wonderful soothing effect on her, not only to dull the pain in her ankle, but to make her feel more comfortable in having Mike wait on her like this.

She looked up at him now, her smile wobbly. "This is good wine. Do you mind if I have another?"

Mike looked at the empty glass in surprise, then refilled it. "You probably should go a little slow with this stuff. Especially since you haven't eaten for a while."

Mary smiled. That was nice. He was being solicitous. But she was fine. "I'm very fine, Mike, thank you," she said aloud. When her words reached her ears they were light and fuzzy, floating like a wavy banner in the breeze. That was the way she felt, like a waving banner, and it was a nice, delicious feeling. She laughed lightly. When she focused back on Mike, she saw he had moved to the fireplace and was leaning over, stoking the logs so that huge leaps of fire darted up against the stone. Lovely, she thought. It was all so lovely. And she took another drink of the delicious-tasting wine. She kept her eyes on Mike, on the bend of his back and the broad shoulders that moved beneath his shirt as he put the fire iron back in its stand. And she watched as he walked across the room until he was nearly out of sight. He certainly had a nice way of walking, she thought. And then she heard his voice, and for a minute she thought he was talking to her. But then her eyes focused in on the phone and she watched and saw his lips moving. "No, tomorrow night maybe..." she heard him say. And then, "Yeah, it'll be great to see you, too. I'm awfully glad you're back. Good night, Franny."

Mary took another drink of wine. She was eavesdropping. Shameful. She was being shameful.

And Mike was calling Franny.

Mike returned with another basket of crackers. "Here, Mary, why don't you have some more crackers?"

"Does Franny like crackers?" she asked. And then she felt the tiny beads of perspiration break out on her forehead and her throat. There was someone inside of her, a stranger, asking these things, saying things Mary Shields would never ever say. She was never overtly nosy. She raked her fingers through her hair. "Sorry. Real sorry, Mike," she said. She tried to smile as she talked, but she was so tired. The tumble down the hill...the ride out to Mike's...teaching all day... And then she added slowly, "You're a nice man, Mike."

"Thank you. And you don't need to be sorry, Mary. If it had been a private call I would have gone into another room. And sure, I guess Franny likes crackers. She'd like you, too, I think. I'll have to introduce you. Franny is one of my sisters."

Mary was unprepared for the rush of pleasure that swept through her. It nearly made her dizzy. She half closed her eyes and felt the smile that spread, with a life of its own, across her face. "Good. It's good that Franny is your sister."

Mike laughed. "I think so, too."

"Does she live in Chester...Chester...s-h-i-r-e?" Mary said carefully. She couldn't trust her voice. It seemed to be mixing up all the words between her head and the outside air, and pronouncing Chestershire was a major challenge. Mike didn't seem to notice.

"Yes. Franny lives on the other side of town, near my parents. She was on a short trip and just got back into town."

"Oh," Mary said. "I love to travel."

"Franny does, too. It's good for her. She's a great gal, but she tends to take on the worries of the world and traveling loosens her up a little."

"What does she worry about?"

"Anything and anyone."

"Does she worry about you?"

Mike did not answer. Mary's question startled him, until he realized she meant nothing by it, and was already going on to other things. For a minute, there, he thought... But no, the wine had loosened her tongue, and she was saying anything that came into her mind, and was now already moving on to something else. She meant nothing by the question.

"Now you—" she said slowly, pointing one finger at Mike "—you don't seem like the worrying kind."

Mike laughed. "Nope, I'm not. It doesn't do a hell of a lot of good now, does it?"

Mary started to shake her head but the effort was greater than she expected, so she took another drink of wine instead. "I worry sometimes," she said, drawing each word out.

"Well, not tonight, you don't. There's nothing to worry about. And tomorrow you'll be good as new."

"The tumble...it made my head fun feely," she said, oblivious to her words. "I must have hit it."

"Maybe," Mike said, holding back his grin. He moved over beside her on the couch. She looked so young tonight. The wine had wiped away the sophistication that she used to keep people at arm's length. Her hair was slightly mussed and several thick locks tumbled over her forehead. He pushed it back with his fingers.

"Feels good," she murmured, resting her head back against the cushions and closing her eyes. "Fingers...so cool."

"How does the ankle feel now?"

"Much, much better, Mike." She used her hand to gesture and then dropped it into Mike's lap.

He squirmed.

"Mike, I think you are a good friend...already.... I don't have many friends, you know."

"Now why's that? A woman as interesting and beautiful as you—" He took her hand in his to remove it from more dangerous contact and took a long breath. It had been a long time since he had been aroused this quickly. And the damnable thing was that Mary had absolutely no idea what effect she was having on him.

"I had a best friend once, when I was a little girl. Her name was Suzanne. Everyone . . . said she wasn't real. . . ."

Mary's voice was so soft now that Mike could barely make out what she was saying.

"What?" he asked, and she answered by leaning closer to him, resting her head on his shoulder. "This feels so good, Mike. No . . . *you* feel so good. So steady . . . and so near . . ."

He could not see her face now; he could only hear the slow, throaty sound of her voice and smell the clean scent of her hair. And then her breathing slowed, and while Mike tried to concentrate on the cool, neutral wall across the room, Mary Shields fell sound asleep.

Hours later she stirred, her mind still playing with sleep. One arm was curled around a pillow, the other resting on top of a mountain of softness.

She forced her eyes open and for a moment Mary had no idea where she was. Slowly, her surroundings registered.

She was on Michael's couch, stretched out, and covered with a down comforter that puffed up above her like a cumulus cloud. One foot was resting on a soft pillow and the only light in the room was that from the flickering flames of the fire in the hearth.

She rolled her head slightly on the pillow and it was then that she saw him. His back was half turned to her, his bare shoulders bent as he quietly coaxed the fire to life.

Mary's heart stopped. He was gazing intently into the fire now, one forearm resting on his knee, a shock of hair falling over his forehead. He wore the same jeans he had had on yesterday, and nothing else. There was a soft glow about him from the fire that heightened the angles of his cheekbones, the golden skin of his shoulders and back. In the low, dancing light of the fire, Mike's handsomeness was startling.

He had done this for her, fitted her into the cushions of his couch, covered her and made her comfortable for the night, and she couldn't remember any of it. He had *cared* for her. Mary felt a huge lump grow in her throat. She swallowed around it and burrowed deeper into the couch. The emotion that engulfed her made no sense, but it was nonetheless real and stinging in its poignancy. She squeezed her eyes closed and fought the prickle of tears. But it was only when she heard him move, felt the shadow of his body coming toward her, that she calmed herself. With great strength of will she lay still, her eyes closed, her breathing slowed.

She could smell the familiar scent of him as he bent over her, and she thought she even heard his smile. He pulled the blanket up a fraction of an inch to just below her chin, his knuckles brushing lightly against her skin. He bent over and whispered something. And in the next breath he was walking away, off into the stillness of the house.

It was much later, when the fire had faded to a soft glow and Mary could see the first faint blush of morning beyond the long windows, that Mike's whispered words registered. *I commit you to my mind's eye, Mary Shields,* he had said. *A place of honor for a beautiful friend...*

And that was all. A cryptic whispered message.

And when she finally drifted back into sleep some time later, the words faded away into her memory; so that days later, when she recalled them, they became something she dreamed, romantic utterances that made her smile because she herself must have conjured them up.

Chapter Five

The sense of well-being that Mary had felt when she finally drifted off to sleep disappeared quickly the next morning.

"Hi," Mike said from across the room. He was standing at the wall of windows opposite her, drinking coffee from a thick mug.

"Hi, yourself," Mary mumbled. Her hand went to her tousled hair, which she tried unsuccessfully to push back into place.

"Sleep well?"

"Yes, thank you."

"Coffee?"

Mary nodded and Mike disappeared for a minute, returning with a second mug. "Here," he said, putting it into her hand and wrapping her fingers around it. "You don't seem quite awake."

"I wake up slowly," she murmured. Then she added, "and usually alone."

"Now that's a shame, a woman as lovely as you." His crooked smile was completely disarming.

Mary started to move, then felt the tightness in her ankle and grimaced.

"How's the foot?"

"Fine, thanks," she said, and tried to prove it by slipping it from beneath the feathery comforter. "Ouch!" she said, as it hit the floor.

"It'll be sore for a few days. But the swelling has gone down some."

He lowered himself on one knee and lifted her ankle with the palm of his hand. His hands were so large and the movement so gentle that Mary was awed for a moment at the contrast. And then she realized she was holding her breath. It was released in a whoosh.

Mike looked up at the sound.

Mary smiled self-consciously.

Mike grinned back. Then he sat back on his heels. "You want to go home, don't you?"

She nodded. "I'm not used to this, to imposing myself on people, taking over their homes, drinking too much of their wine—having them care for me—"

"Quiet, Mary, I'll allow none of that in my home. I'm glad you came. And even more happy that you stayed. It was nice having someone here when I woke up. I always thought it was such a waste to make a whole pot of coffee for one person."

His eyes were twinkling and worked their magic on Mary. She began to relax. "Okay. Glad to oblige," she said. "But I need to go. I have a stack of short stories to read, and some writing of my own to do. Weekends are too short."

"Fair enough. From the looks of your ankle, you'll be able to hobble around okay, although I wouldn't try a bank robbery—speedy escapes are out for a while."

Mary agreed. And then she made her way, slowly and carefully and using the wall for support, to a large, sunny bathroom off the master bedroom. Mike had put out thick white towels and although she protested at first Mary took him up on his offer for her to shower there. She felt grungy and wrinkled, and the flood of hot water was a welcome respite and exactly what she needed to restore her to her old self.

A short while later she found Mike sitting in the living room, his feet up on the coffee table, reading the paper. He looked up at her with pleasure. "You look like Venus rising."

"And about time, don't you think?" Mary said cheerily, unsure of the similarities between herself and the naked goddess. She looked over in the direction of the kitchen,. "I smell something—"

Mike got up. "The lady has finely honed senses. Good—" He cupped her elbow in his palm and helped her into the sunny kitchen. There was a glassed-in area that extended directly out into the trees. And it was there he sat her, at a round oak table with two colorful mats neatly placed and a heavy piece of pottery overflowing with fresh wildflowers in the center.

"Breakfast is served," Mike said with a bow.

"But—"

"Sh-h-h—" His fingers closed over her lips. "I treat my drop-ins right, lovely lady, so no arguments." With great fanfare he swept a napkin onto her lap and then moved across the room to the huge restaurant-sized stove.

"What can I do?" she asked. "I can't just sit here while you çook."

"Why not? Converse with the birds, read the paper, talk to me. No, I have it, *sing* with me!"

"You're crazy, Mike."

With one hand, Mike dramatically cracked eggs into a pan. They sizzled, as they spread out across the hot fat. "Crazy, she says," he murmured, and then, while he lifted and shook the cast-iron skillet with the ease of a weight lifter, he began to sing: *I'm as corny as Kansas in August...*

Mary watched him in astonishment for a minute, while his deep voice filled the room and then, surprising herself, she joined in, her light, lilting voice carried along on the cushion of his baritone and the bright laughter in his eyes. They sang on, one song after another, and it wasn't until Mike settled two heaping plates of eggs on the table in front of her that Mary realized it was one of the few times in her life she had ever sung in front of another person. The thought made her feel giddy and free.

"There," Mike said, pulling out a chair and joining her. "These eggs are great. Eat up."

Mary's face was flushed, her eyes bright from the singing. "Mike, I don't know what to make of you. But I certainly like you."

"And you don't let yourself do that easily, do you, Mary?"

He was serious, but far too kind to put her on the spot, so he followed up his question with a grin and the insistence that she try some apple butter on the thick toasted muffin he had slipped onto her plate.

Finally, stuffed and more relaxed than she could remember being for a long time, Mary reluctantly pushed herself away from the table. "I hate to do it, but I have to go. Let's get these dishes done first and—"

"Nope." Mike looked at his wristwatch. "No time for that. Emily will do them when she comes in to move my dust around. I have to get going, too."

"You work on Saturdays?"

Mike grabbed Mary's sweater from a brass hook near the door and draped it over her shoulders. "Sometimes I do. But today I have other things to do. Franny needs some work done at her house, I need to go to the market, and one of my nieces is having a birthday party. I said I'd drop by."

Mary listened as she hobbled out to Mike's car. It was all so domestic. Here he was, a thirty-six-year-old bachelor, with a magnetic appeal that awed her sometimes, and he was leading this odd sort of life. It didn't make sense, but it seemed to make him happy, so who was she to judge?

"Boring, right?" Mike was looking at her, again reading into her mind, sorting through her private thoughts.

"Yes," she said honestly. "And yet you strike me as being one of the least boring people I know."

His laughter spun around in the autumn air. It was deep and alive, a billowing kind of laughter. "Mary, the problem with you is that you don't have enough behind you, enough variety. You have the life you lived in upstate New York, and you have your imagination."

"That's right. That's exactly right," she said. She had tried to explain that to her agent once, and he hadn't understood. Mike opened the car door and waited until she settled herself inside, then pushed the door closed and strode around the car. He folded his long legs into the driver's side and continued his train of thought. "That's why my life sounds boring to you. By itself, maybe it would be. But my past is cluttered with all sorts of things, and I think that colors the present."

"So what I need is more *past* to color my present."

Mike laughed. "Something like that, I guess."

"Well, I agree completely. And that's exactly what I intend to get. I'm going to grab at everything, feed on life, see everything there is to see."

Mike listened while her throaty voice carried them both off to all sorts of worlds that Mary dreamed about. He'd been in and out of some of them himself—the traveling, the South of France, plays in England, the walks along the ocean's shore and midnight strolls through teeming, alive cities, bumping shoulders with vagrants and movie stars.

"But no matter how much color I find," Mary was saying beside him, "I don't think it will ever be enough to make me then want to sit back in a town like Chestershire for the rest of my life. No," her head rolled back and forth along the leather of his car seat, "I can't imagine that ever happening to me."

Then she smiled, a small smile, and wondered why there was a slight pain in her stomach when it was her ankle that she had injured.

THE PATTERN OF MARY and Mike's days evolved without conscious thought.

Most days they met on campus for lunch. Mike brought enormous sandwiches that left Mary feeling full and happy, and they sat beneath a grove of twisted oak trees and talked. That was one of the things Mary liked the most about Mike, she decided—the talking. She found herself talking on and on about herself, about life, about her writing and her hopes and dreams. Sometimes she felt as if she were making up for all those years when she had had no one to talk to but the pink-flowered walls of her room.

When Mary tried to analyze the reasons for her openness with Mike, she came up with three. First, she and Mike were far too different in careers and in philosophies of life to have anything complicated develop between them, even in spite of the sexual tension that often existed when their bodies accidentally rubbed together, or when Mike wrapped his arm around her shoulder, or when he looked at her with those incredibly blue eyes that stared right down into the middle of her soul. Secondly, she and Mike were both well aware that they would most likely never see one another once the workshop was over and she went back to her 'other life,' as Mike called it. And thirdly, well, thirdly, he was just easy to be with, easy and safe.

Safe. Yes, that was it. She was safe with Mike.

"ALL RIGHT NOW," Mary said one crisp autumn noon, as Mike scooped up the crushed waxed-paper wrappings of their sandwiches and stuffed them into a bag, "this is the part that's driving me absolutely crazy. I can't seem to move the story along. Would you help me with this, Mike?"

She had her glasses on, large, round tortoiseshell glasses that sometimes slipped down her nose and that Mike found absolutely charming. "What's that?" he asked, smiling slightly at the gesture he was now so familiar with, the narrow fingers pushing the glasses up while her eyes widened, looking at him as if she were surprised, suddenly, that she wasn't alone.

"When Nicholas falls into the lake—"

"Nicholas?"

Mary frowned. She jabbed her pencil into the pad of paper that was settled in her lap, but her eyes remained on Mike. "Mike, you're out in left field today. Nicholas, my protagonist."

"Oh, sure, *Nicholas*. I know him. Go ahead." Mike listened carefully. Her characters were so real to her, people she was creating, people taking on lives of their own. She even asked him to read some stuff, some short stories she was playing with, and she had never, *ever* let anyone do that before, she informed him earnestly.

Mike liked it, liked listening to her and seeing her talent slowly unravel before him along with the words of the manuscript. But what he liked most of all was having Mary unravel herself. When he had first met her that day in the Laundromat she had been lovely, shy and underneath all that uptight. But slowly, day by day, the protective shield had fallen away, until now she talked to him with a kind of abandon. "I wonder if writing is like that," Mike said out loud.

"Like what?" Mary slipped off her glasses.

"Sorry. I was thinking out loud." He dropped the remnants of their lunch into the trash can and walked back over to her. "I wonder if characters in your novels and short stories emerge slowly, like you've emerged to me."

Mary pulled her brows together in thought. Then she answered, "Probably. You pull off the layers page by page and finally the soul is there." And then she lowered her head so suddenly that her glasses fell into her lap.

Mike leaned down and tipped up her chin with strong, blunt fingers. Finally she met his gaze. He was smiling at her. "It's okay," he said. "I like it. And each layer is a delightful surprise."

Mary took his hand and pulled herself to her feet, then brushed the leaves off her tan slacks. "Time to get back," she said with unusual brusqueness. "My class will be waiting."

Mike's eyes twinkled. "Okay. I've got things to do, too."

"Pipes to fix, doors to unstick—"

"Some of that. Some other stuff. I've got to meet with some faculty over at the business school. That's why I got so spiffed up."

Mary took in the khaki pants and knit shirt. She smiled. "Oh, I see. Asking for business advice?"

"Nope. Talking over other possibilities."

Mike took her hand and they started walking along the path, back toward the building that housed the writers' institute.

"Possibilities . . ." Mary repeated.

"Yeah, life's full of them, don't you think?" Mike's strides were so long and purposeful that Mary had to hurry to keep up with him.

"I suppose it is."

"Well, my favorite possibility, looks like we're here—" He nodded toward the door of her building where a small group of students were gathering. "And looks like your young, impressionable minds are eager to gobble up your wisdom."

"What—"

"How about dinner tonight?"

Mary slipped on her glasses and looked at him closely. "Mike—about this business-school meeting . . . ?"

"It'll be over in time. How about dinner at my folks'? Pick you up at seven." He leaned over, planted a chaste kiss on her forehead and was off.

Mary stared after him. Her head felt cluttered, a hodgepodge of puzzle pieces that didn't fit together at all. She shook her head, pushed a smile in place and walked off toward the waiting students.

"OKAY, LITTLE BROTHER, what's going on?"

Franny Gibson Nelson stood in the middle of the Gibsons' large, warm kitchen, her small fists dug into shapely hips. She glared up at her brother.

"You like Mary?" he asked. He took a beer from the refrigerator and flipped back the tab.

"Like her? That doesn't matter diddly squat, but, yes, I like her." Franny took the beer from his hand.

"What does matter?" Mike asked, rummaging around for another one.

"You. You look moonstruck."

"Too many soaps, Franny."

"You know I don't have time to watch soaps. I want to know who this gal is and why you look at each other the way you do and what part she plays in your life and—"

"—whether we're sleeping together and if we want two kids or five."

"Exactly!"

Mike laughed. "I love you, Franny, but you really do have this streak in you that makes mountains out of molehills. Mary and I have become good friends. Purely platonic friends."

"There is no such thing. Not between different sexes." Franny picked up a piece of french bread, left over from the enormous dinner they had finished a half hour before, and began munching on it.

Mike poured a glass of tonic water for Mary and thought about Franny's comment. Finally he said, "I used to think that. But this thing with Mary is different. We both know she's leaving here in a few weeks, we both know we want to live in totally different worlds. I know I'm a major catch, Franny, but I really think she's only interested in my ability to fix leaky faucets."

Franny socked him in the hard plane of his gut. "Catch, my foot. Who'd want you, Gibs, you're a crock of—"

"Franny, and you a mother of three!"

"And mothers are taught to look for things like lust in a guy's eyes."

Mike was laughing fully now. "So that's what you see in my eyes, huh? Could be worse."

Franny sobered up immediately. "Don't joke about your eyes, Mike." She paused, took a long drink of her beer and looked up at him with unabashed love. "Does Mary know about your eyes?"

Mike shrugged. "No. No reason, really. Like I said, Franny, she's leaving in a couple of weeks. There's been no reason to unload on her. Besides—" he pinched Franny's cheek, "—we have *far* more interesting things to talk about. All those lusty looks and unleashed passion don't lead to medical talk.''

While Franny moaned, he took her elbow and steered her out of the kitchen. "Come on. Let's get out there before Mom has Mary looking at the albums."

But they were too late.

"And this is before the music building was built and we used to picnic with the little ones down near the stream," Marie Gibson was saying, her soft, lovely voice drifting through the room.

She and Mary were seated side-by-side on a large, comfortable sofa. In front of them, sprawled across an oak coffee table, was an assortment of leather-bound photo albums.

Mike groaned. "Mom, what do you have against Mary? She minded all her manners, had seconds on your pie—give the woman a break!"

Mike's father, a friendly, quiet man with eyes that sparkled as readily as his son's, waved Mike into a chair. "Don't even try to stop her, Mike. Mary made the major mistake of commenting on the fact that we look alike."

"So now we'll explore it from all angles," Franny said. "The diaper angle, the baseball angle, the—"

"Oh, hush, all of you," said diminutive Marie Gibson. She was a pretty gray-haired lady with the lively movements of a woman much younger, and she ruled her family with a solid hand. "I'm showing Mary some things about Indiana she never knew."

"And was afraid to ask, no doubt," Franny said. She squeezed her father's shoulder lightly while she talked.

Mary watched them all, recording the gestures and small signs of affection that flowed throughout the house like warm honey. They genuinely *liked* each other, that was obvious. And they were physical in their affection, sometimes playful, sometimes not. When she and Mike had come into the house a couple hours earlier, Marie Gibson, after kissing Mike fondly, had actually pushed his hair out of his eyes. And then she had smiled at Mary and hugged her warmly, a gesture that Mary knew was as sincere as all the rest of the affection that flowed through the big house. Mary had stood there while Marie hugged her, she had smiled, but she hadn't been sure how to respond, and the feeling left her uncomfortable, out of her element.

Mary sat back on the sofa now, as Mike's mother and Franny debated the identity of an old woman in one of the pictures. Mike and his father were discussing some construction at the college and Mary let her mind wander from the warm, comfortable Indiana living room to thoughts of her own father. She wondered if siblings would have made a difference in her life...in *their* lives together. Maybe things would have been different. Maybe then she would have felt like a family. She tried to imagine her father sitting where Mike's father sat. Stan Gibson was scratching the ears of a long-eared mutt named Hoosier, who seemed attached to the senior Gibson's feet. Smoke curled up from Stan's pipe and passed by twinkling eyes, *loving* eyes, Mary thought. He was sitting there loving all of them; she could almost feel it. She felt the sting of the tears before the fact registered in her mind and the warm liquid blurred her vision.

It might have been a disaster, an unexpected flood that would have shamed Mary in front of this family she barely knew. But a ruckus out on the front lawn jarred her back before any damage was done and she was able to wipe away the moisture without anyone seeing.

"Looks like the kids are back," Stan Gibson said.

Franny's three children, her husband and another of Mike's sisters and her children had left shortly after dinner to bike downtown for frozen yogurt, which they promised to bring back for everyone. They had all embraced Mary as if she had grown up with them in the shade of the enormous rain tree in the backyard. Her writing was appreciated but not fawned over; it was *her* they were interested in, and they bombarded her with questions about where she lived, what she did, and whether or not she had ever been robbed in the city of vice and excitement.

Franny's oldest daughter, Ella, was fourteen and was immediately besotted with Mary and the fact that she lived in New York. Ella, Franny explained with loving humor, was thinking about being a great stage star and Ella then told Mary about the school play in which she had a challenging role, one that would certainly stretch her as an actress. Her brother Alex, fifteen, handsome and awkward, did not say much but he spent most of the dinner looking at Mary.

They all came in now like the winds before an Indiana tornado, and while Alex fell to the floor near the television, making sure Mary was in his direct line of vision, Ella plopped down next to Mary, depositing a white bag on the table. "White chocolate mousse," she announced proudly. "My favorite. You'll love it, Mary."

The younger children tore into the kitchen to get out bowls and silverware while Ella entertained the rest with backstage stories about her school production. Before long there were small, sleeping lumps in front of the television and Michael's dad was trying to stifle a yawn.

"Time to be off," Michael announced, and while his mother stuffed foil-wrapped mounds of leftovers into a paper sack for him, he and Mary said goodbye to the rest of the Gibson clan.

Mary was quiet on the ride home. She felt inundated with a kind of closeness that disturbed her. They had all hugged her goodbye, along with promising to show her more of Indiana before she went back to New York. She had felt overwhelmed by their acceptance. Overwhelmed and confused.

"Well?" Mike asked finally.

"Your mother is a wonderful cook."

"Thank you. That's why I came back to Indiana. That's why I took you over there, too."

"I'm sorry, Mike, I just don't know what to say."

"Hey, Mary, I'm not asking for an evaluation." Mike patted her thigh briefly. "I just wondered if you had a good time. You seemed to be, and they all liked you."

"Of course I had a good time. How could I not? Your family is wonderful."

And then the tears began to fall down her face. They came in rivers and her voice gave way to the emotion that had been building up inside her since the moment she had walked through the wide, welcoming doors of the Gibsons' home.

Mike frowned and tried to concentrate on his driving. He had plenty of sisters, plus an ex-wife and an assortment of other relationships. He should know what to do, understand the situation. But Mary Shields stymied him. She defied the laws for females that he had compiled over the years. She didn't follow the rules. So he concentrated on the darkness falling across the town, opened up the window, and he hummed.

Later that night, Mike stood alone on his wooden deck and looked out into the blackness. Beyond was the woods, but in the deep black of night its presence was only made real through scent and feel. He could *feel* it, feel its vast greenness and damp, leafy depth. Standing there usually worked an immediate magic on Mike, filling his head with the odor of pine and his soul with the magic of nature.

But tonight it didn't work its magic on him; tonight his thoughts were on Mary Shields.

When they had reached her bungalow earlier, she was out of the car and inside before he could move. No need to walk her to the door, she'd tossed over her shoulder. And then, murmuring something about an early day, she'd disappeared, swollen eyes and all. She had never made reference to the crying, nor had he. It had simply happened.

Being with a beautiful woman usually assured Mike of a good night's sleep. But tonight, seeing the raw vulnerability in Mary Shields's tears, made that utterly impossible.

Chapter Six

"It's writer's block, Mike, plain and simple."

"Mary, nothing about you is plain and simple. Besides, I thought you didn't believe in writer's block."

"I don't believe in it happening to other people. But it's *me*, Mike. It's happened to me."

Mike was lying on his back, his head beneath the sink in the kitchen of the small house that served as Professor Atwood's office and home. "Hand me that screwdriver, will you please?" he mumbled.

"Mike, I don't know where to go for help. You're the only person I can think of."

"I'd be glad to help, Mary—" Mike grasped the top of the sink and pulled himself out. His forearms bulged beneath the effort. He sat up and grinned at her. "Except I don't know what the hell you're talking about. You've convinced me that writer's block is a convention made up by writers to explain their laziness. So how can I help you get rid of something that you've made up?"

"I don't know." She nibbled on her bottom lip.

She was sitting in the corner of the kitchen, her legs crossed as nimbly as a gymnast's and her lap full of loose sheets of paper. Her hair was pulled back and tied at her neck, but several strands had pulled loose and framed her face now in shadowy wisps.

"You're a puzzling one, Mary Shields." Mike fumbled around in his toolbox until he found a larger wrench, then slid back under the sink.

Mary watched him for a few minutes in companionable silence, then went back to her papers. She had come over during a two-hour break to bring Mike a sandwich. And she had taken to talking through aspects of her novel with Mike, finding it helped her clarify her own thought to muse out loud. But mostly she had come because she wanted to see him, wanted to be sure her strange behavior after they left his parents hadn't become something to stumble around before they could be friends again.

But explaining her feelings was another thing. She couldn't even explain them to herself. She had liked his family. Every one of them. They had been warm and gracious and accepting of her simply because Mike liked her. That was good enough for them. And for some unearthly reason, that kind acceptance unnerved her.

"You still there?" Mike peeked out from beneath the sink.

She nodded. Mike went back to tinkering with the pipe.

"My family liked you, Mary," he said quietly.

"Yes," she said, almost in a whisper. "They were very nice to me."

"They wouldn't call it being nice. They could call it Hoosier hospitality."

Mary was silent. She thought of his mother, and how she had hugged Mary before she left, making her promise that if she needed anything at all, Marie was at the end of the phone. She thought of being embraced by those strong, womanly arms.

Mike went on. "You know, I think my family is great. But sometimes they—me, too, I suppose—come on a little strong. My folks have never met a stranger, and they assume everyone else is that way, too."

Mike groped around with one hand out for a larger screwdriver, then continued. "Their easy affection is hard on some people. It can seem overwhelming."

Mary doodled on the sheet of paper. How did he know that? How was he able to figure out exactly how she felt, when she herself had such a hard time with it? "Well," she said at last, "I think your whole family is lovely. I guess . . . I guess I'm simply not used to it. My father wasn't very affectionate and it scares me a little. He loved me, I know that. He loved me a great deal. But there weren't a lot of hugs in our house."

"There're all sorts of ways of showing love and affection," Mike answered.

"Yes, there are."

"But it was your father's loss not to know how huggable a daughter he had." He said it lightly, coming out from beneath the sink for a minute to grin at her. "And I'll be more than obliged to make up for it, given the time and opportunity, ma'am."

Mary looked up from her doodling and smiled at him. "Thanks, kind sir."

He saluted her with a wrench, then scooted back beneath the sink. Mary looked down at the piece of paper in her lap. *Mike* was spelled out in loops and curls around the border of the page. She smiled at the games her subconscious was playing on her. And then she changed the subject.

"Mike, tell me something," she said. "Why did you move away from Indiana?"

"Oh, probably it was a combination of things. To see new sights, meet new people. But also there were opportunities in California not available to me here or in Boston."

Mary frowned. "What do you mean?"

"I was in a different business then and California was the place to be."

"What business?"

Mike gave the pipe a final tap with his wrench and then pulled himself up. He began to wash his hands. "I was in the computer business."

"Oh?"

He looked at her over his shoulder. "Yeah. I started a company out in California. We made software programs for business. Specialized kinds of things."

Mary continued to watch him, but she didn't speak. It was finally making sense to her. Mike had had a business and it must have failed, so he came back to

Indiana. And she had been about as sensitive as a slug and forced him to tell her about his failure. She lowered her head and stared at the papers on her lap.

Mike wiped his hands on a rag and dropped it into a sack, then closed his tool kit. "There, looks like I'm done here." He held out a hand to help her up from the floor.

"Mike, I'm sorry. I was nosing into your past again. I had no right."

Mike looked at her with a strange expression on his face. "Mary," he said finally, "you live too much in your mind. What is all this crap about rights and being nosy? I've told you before, if you ask me something I don't want to tell you, I won't, but there's no shame in asking now, is there?"

"But I shouldn't have probed about the company. Obviously there were problems or—"

Then, realizing the logic of Mary's thought, Mike laughed. He took her shoulders between the large palms of his hands and said, "Mary, the only problems I had were wondering which offer to take. I was offered so much money for my company when I decided to sell it that I was embarrassed."

They were standing close without realizing it and Mary took a quick breath. "You—"

He lifted her chin with two fingers and looked into her eyes. "You thought I went bankrupt or something, didn't you?" His eyes were laughing.

She nodded slightly.

"Nope, no bankruptcy. You're always looking for an interesting story and I hate to disappoint you, but this one is very undramatic, Mary. Boring."

"So you sold a successful company."

"Yes. And for want of a better word, I'm rich."

He was leading her out of the professor's house now, out onto the busy street. "Satisfied?" He grinned down at her.

Mary ignored the grin. "And you took all your money and got a job as a carpenter at an Indiana college."

"Right. Which also hired you—but that may end real soon if you don't get back to work." He nodded across the street. Students were filing into the vine-covered building. Several waved at Mary.

"Okay, Gibson," she said. "I'll go. But this isn't the end of it, you know." She hadn't moved and neither had Mike. They stood together on the sidewalk, facing each other with only a small slice of air between them.

He looked down at her, then lifted one hand and lightly touched her hair. "Good. I'm glad it's not the end of it."

Mary's heart began to beat faster. It was the confusion, she told herself. The craziness of Mike being rich. The inconsistencies that peppered his life. "I guess I'd better go," she said. Her voice came out in a thin trickle and then it cracked.

Mike knew he was going to kiss her, and he knew it made no more sense than it had the last time he'd done it. But sense didn't seem to have anything to do with the feelings Mary stirred up in him. He lowered his head that one final inch and he found Mary waiting for him.

A small moan escaped her lips, and then she responded with a gentle pressure of her own. Mike's hand lifted, his fingers threading through the silken strands of her hair. With slow, deliberate movements, he explored the moist curve of her lips, and then, when Mary parted her lips slightly, Michael responded and his tongue slipped within.

Jolts of pleasure shot through Mary with such unexpected force she thought she was going to lose her balance and her arms lifted instinctively and wound around Mike's neck.

"Well, hello there." Professor Atwood's gravelly, delighted voice fell on them from some distant spot. "I can presume the sink is fixed, Michael?"

Mike pulled slowly away, but his hand lingered on Mary's neck. He looked over at the elderly professor and smiled. "Works like a charm, professor."

"A charm. Yes, indeed. I'm sure it did, Michael." And then he disappeared into the house, his deep chuckles rolling down the short strip of sidewalk behind him.

"The man is going to think I'm a nymphomaniac, Michael! Every time he sees me it looks like I'm attacking you." Mary sought to steady herself.

"Are you?"

"Of course not!" She frowned at him and hoped it covered up the tiny beads of moisture on her neck and face.

"Well, okay. But it's fine with me if you want to."

She looked up into his smiling eyes. "Michael, what's going on here?"

"Damned if I know, but I'm not complaining."

Mary shook her head. The cool breeze cleared her head. She looked up at him.

"Whatever is going on, Mary, I don't want it to ruin your seminar." He turned her around slowly, until she faced the classroom building across the way. And then he lowered his head and brushed a kiss along the soft skin at the back of her neck. "They're waiting for you, Mary," he whispered.

And then, with a small wave to the gaggle of students who had collected at the casement windows in Mary's classroom to watch, Mike turned and strode on down the street.

Chapter Seven

It had been an incredible dream, filled to the brim with color and movement. At its center, with a spontaneous grace that sent Mike's sleeping head spinning, was Mary Shields.

Mike moaned when the shrill ring of the telephone scattered the sensual images across his mind and out into the black oblivion of the night. One hand reached from beneath the covers and groped blindly for the phone.

"Hello," he mumbled finally. His voice was thick with sleep.

"Mike, it's Mary."

The dream started to come back now, the colors forming and the slender woman with the black hair taking her place right back in the center of it all.

"Michael? Are you awake?"

And then the dream was reduced to sound—the lovely sound of Mary's voice.

"Are you awake?" the voice repeated.

"Hm-m-m," Mike said slowly. "The answers to that question are limited."

Mary's laughter was low, hesitant. "This was so bold of me, to call you like this."

"Bold is sometimes nice," he said, his mind fighting off the fogginess.

"It's about that writer's block—"

"Whose what?" Mike rolled over slowly and looked toward the window. Beyond it was darkness. He fumbled for the light switch. "Um-m . . . Mary, what time is it?"

"I don't know for sure," Mary said. "Maybe I should have checked before I called. That was thoughtless of me."

"*Bold . . . thoughtless . . .* this can't be the Mary Shields I know."

She smiled.

Finally Mike's fingers found the switch and a beam of soft yellowish light fell across his bed. He glanced at the bedside clock. "Mary, darlin', it's three-thirty in the morning."

"Oh, my."

The cool night air circled around Mike, down beneath the plaid blanket, and sent shivers along his bare skin. He began to wake up.

"Mike, I'm sorry. I had no idea . . ."

"No, it's okay. You've come into my bedroom at three-thirty in the morning. Don't ever apologize for that. Are you okay? Where are you?"

"I'm fine and I'm home."

"Home. All right, that's good." Her words were coming more clearly now. He smiled. Did she know about his dream? "Were you having trouble sleeping?" he asked.

"No. I was trying to write. But I can't. It's still with me, Michael."

"Who?"

"The writer's block."

"Oh, *that*." Mike stretched in the wide bed.

"I thought maybe you could talk me out of it."

Mike smiled. "Okay, Mary. Then what we need to do is get comfortable here, and then we can explore it a little." The sheet was cool against his bare skin, but the thought of Mary on the other end of the line sent a rush of warmth down his spine and the cold dissolved like ice cubes on a summer's day.

"Yes," she said.

"Okay. But I need to have you in my mind, first. You know, situated. Mental image. The magic writer's-block-destroying technique is useless if the mental picture isn't well focused. Are you in bed?"

Mary's middle-of-the-night laughter was low and throaty and sent unexpected delight shooting through Michael. "No," she said, "but I'm close to it. I'm sitting on the blue chaise in my bedroom."

"What do you have on?"

"Michael!"

"You're naked?"

"Of course not. It's just such a . . ."

"...a personal question. Yeah, but when I get a phone call at three in the morning, I figure I can take certain liberties. I mean this is an intimate thing we have here, Mary, and the task ahead of us is a formidable one."

"Of course," Mary said. She was smiling, too. There was something lovely about having Mike on the end of the phone line, as close to her as a heartbeat, yet safely distanced across town in his own bed. Her imagination began to frolic and she let it go, unimpeded, feeling safe and secure in the darkness of the night. "Okay, Mike," she said, "I'm wrapped up in a pink terry-cloth robe—which I believe you've seen—and my hair is mussed, my feet are bare and cold. And I'm surrounded by dozens of yellow pads of paper, most of them blank."

Mike played with the images. He wanted to feel the soft, curling strands of her hair framing her face. He wanted to take her feet in the palms of his hands and gently rub warmth into them. He wanted to loosen the sash on the thick terry-cloth robe. Aloud he coughed and then said, "Okay. You're coming into focus. Now let's get to work."

Mary hugged her knees up to her chest. His voice was losing the sleepy tones, but she could still picture him there in his bed, his midnight blue eyes trying to focus, his chin covered with the shadow of a night's beard. She wondered what *he* had on, but she was afraid to ask.

"Want to know what I have on?" he asked.

"Not fair. You can't jump into my head that way, Michael, not from that far away."

"I knew it. It's that writer's curiosity. Well, I'll tell you—"

"No!" Mary felt the heat building up inside of her. She pressed her legs together.

"Okay, I'll leave it to your imagination." He chuckled softly.

"I called about Nicholas, the man I told you about—"

"Ah, yes, Nicholas. Although I must confess, Mare, I rather resent you bringing another man into this right now. I mean here I am, naked as a jaybird, pulled out of an incredible dream, still drowsy with sleep . . . and there you are in your pink robe, your hair falling across that lovely smooth forehead, your—"

"Michael, stop," she said in a whisper. He was naked. Why did he have to tell her that? But what did it matter? If she had allowed herself to go any further, that was how he would have been in her mind anyway. She saw him as clearly now as if he were in her own bed a few feet away.

He was laying back against a wide bank of pillows, his chest bare and tan and muscular, covered with black springy hairs that formed a pattern across his ribs. A sheet was pulled up partway, resting across his abdomen, smooth and white, and the phone would be wedged between his ear and a plump pillow, and, oh, yes, there would be laughter spilling out of those incredible eyes, laughter and warmth and delight. "I couldn't write..." she said. "I couldn't move my thoughts. I thought maybe you could help."

"Sure, never let it be said I left a maiden in distress at three-plus in the morning, especially one as enchanting as you. So Nicholas is giving you trouble, is he?"

"Terrible trouble." Mary snuggled down deeper into the cushions of the chaise and pulled a light throw over her.

One recent night, as an autumn moon lit their way, she and Mike had wandered along the winding paths of the campus and she had told him all about her character Nicholas. He was an innocent young man from Idaho who had been raised by three aunts. At seventeen he had found himself alone for the first time in his life.

"Maybe you're trying too hard to give this Nick character," Mike said. "Maybe he simply doesn't have it, at least not yet." He closed his eyes and leaned his head back into the fat pillows.

"But he has to, Mike. He has to or he won't survive, at least not in my book."

"He can grow, can't he? Maybe he needs time to be weak before he can be strong."

Mary thought about that, but she was finding it increasingly difficult to concentrate on a man with weak character who came from Idaho. What fuzzed her writer's mind and heightened her senses were thoughts of a man with strength and vitality and virility...a man who came from Indiana...a man who...

"Mare? You with me?"

"Absolutely," she said dreamily.

Mike smiled. The wind rustled through the blinds and shook the small lamp shade; it sent sleeping shadows cavorting across the room. He wondered what Mary was wearing under the thick pink robe.

"I think Nicholas was the victim of too much love," Mary said.

"I don't think that's possible. Not if it's genuine."

"How about obsessive?"

"Then it's not real."

"Okay. So the women in his life raised him with an obsessive love."

"Unfortunate fellow."

"And he feels hollow, empty, when he leaves that life behind. Instead of strength, their obsessive love left him with fears and self-doubts. There's nothing to bolster him."

While her soft, sleepy words came across the phone line, Mike thought about his relationship with Mary. He hadn't thought he needed bolstering. He had conquered all his demons and took pride in his independence. But in some way, Mary had provided a kind of support, nevertheless. Perhaps it was simply the comfort of friendship, but there was something about her presence in his life that created a brace, and the thought surprised him. And then suddenly, without warning, the realization that she would leave Chestershire in a few weeks hit him forcefully, and along with it came the clear truth that when she did, she wouldn't walk out of his life easily. He would miss her.

"Michael?" she was saying. "Are you still there or did you fall off to sleep?"

"I'm here, Mary," he said.

"Good. I need you to be there." Her voice had grown soft again.

"What happened to Nicholas?"

"He went to sleep."

"Smart man."

"I think it's all he can do right now. Tomorrow maybe he'll turn into a man."

"Maybe. You know, Mary, I can see the Big Dipper from my window."

"I see lots of stars from here."

"The same ones. Nice, huh? We're looking at the same stars—"

"You're a romantic, Mike."

"Incurable. And you know, the sky is so much more beautiful when there's someone to share it."

"See, you *are* glad I called."

Her voice was dreamy, sleepy, and Michael felt himself intoxicated by the sound of it. He closed his eyes again. Her presence was so real there beside him that he felt he could reach out and rub his hand down the side of her face. Touch her chin, the long white column of her neck, the perfect mounds of her breasts.

They were both silent for a minute, the phone line connecting their spirits as they played with mind images and words and feelings.

"Mike...?" Mary sought him in the stillness.

"Hmmmmm?"

"Are you falling asleep?"

"Asleep? If that means dreaming of a lovely woman, feeling her here beside me...if it means feeling slightly drugged in a wonderful way...then maybe I am."

"You seem so close, Mike."

"I am, darlin'."

Mary burrowed down beneath the blanket, her head sinking into the pillows of the chaise. She closed her eyes and gave in to the stirrings that were growing without warning inside of her. "This is kind of crazy, Mike..."

"I guess...I suppose we should go to sleep—" His voice was strangely thick.

Mary's breathing finally slowed. She felt her body begin to lighten, then relax, and she thought of all the lovely images of the night. Sleep...would the images stay? Would they grow? Would she and Mike be together in sleep...?

Michael snapped off his light and looked out the window. While he watched, the darkness began to fade and the sky lightened, to slate, to dove, to a soft peach, and a short while later the robins and finches and blue jays began to stir in the tangle of woods beyond his deck. The glory of a new day shot through the sky.

Mike shifted the phone against the pillow, then pressed it to his ear and whispered softly into the mouthpiece. "Good morning, my love," he said.

But all that met his ear, just as he knew it would, was the gentle, slow breathing of Mary in sleep.

When Michael awoke the next morning, the world was drenched in crisp autumn sunshine. The sky, a deep, clear azure, hung over his woods like a celestial awning. And there was something else present in the new day, something as real as the sky and the sun: the relationship with Mary Shields had been altered irrevocably.

He stood on the deck in the chilly air, his bare chest numb to the breeze, and took in huge lungfuls of air. The pine scent stung his nostrils and invigorated him. He hooked his thumbs through the belt loops of his jeans. How had it happened? He knew far too much about Mary to have let it; but somehow logic and common sense hadn't entered in, at all. There was a feeling running along his bones that had nothing to do with friendship. And then he laughed, partly out of joy, and partly at the unreality of the whole situation.

He was drowning in a "morning after" feeling—and yet he hadn't so much as touched her.

Chapter Eight

Mike showed up at Mary's door at three in the afternoon the next Saturday and asked her if she had ever played third base.

"Never," Mary assured him.

"That's a shame," said Mike. "It's about time, don't you think?"

Mary assured him she did not, but Mike wouldn't listen. "Wear jeans," he said, "and a sweatshirt. It's kind of cold out there."

"Mike," she protested, "I mean it. Softball is not my game. Besides, it might rain."

"Mary," he said, leaning against the door frame of her bungalow, "you're the writer. And a writer without life's experiences under her belt isn't worthy of the name. And you're wrong—it's not going to rain."

Mike knew the way to get to her, the way to urge her on to do anything. But the truth was, Mary thought, she would have gone anyway; she would have gone just to be with him. If he had suggested a three-legged race in a muddy meadow, she would have walked out the door with him.

The field was behind the college library and Mike told her a bunch of them played there all year long, ignoring seasons. "I mean," he said, leaning so close to her that his breath tickled her neck, "baseball is America. Why just play in spring and summer?" Then he took her hand and led her out into the clearing to meet the *Could Be's* and the *Has Been's*.

"Hey, Stu," Mike said to a tall man walking over to them, "Meet Mary Shields. Mary this is Stu Tolliver, business-school professor." Then he added, "Stu is our leading . . . our leading . . . our leading what, Stu?"

"Leading all-around-in-general everything, you know that, Mike," he said, and then followed it up with a deep, stomach-borne kind of laughter that made Mary like him right away. She liked his wife, Polly, too, a small blond woman who spoke irreverently about anything that popped into her mind. The others ranged from philosophy professors to art teachers to the owner of Nick's Bar and they all greeted Mary warmly, assuring her that both teams needed all the help they could get.

Someone brought up her writing, and it was plain from their comments that these people knew Mike well, and that they had all heard about her from him. The thought warmed her.

Mike watched her chatting easily with his friends. He did not know why it had taken him so long to introduce her to this group. They were all old friends and had become his social life since he had moved back from California. Maybe he was hoarding her, saving her like a special book. Maybe it was because most of these people knew him too well, many having been friends nearly all his life. Maybe that was it, a subconscious need to keep Mary separate from the entirety of his life.

Who knows, but whatever the reason, he was glad he brought her today. She seemed comfortable enough with everyone, and a slow surge of pride swept over him as he saw the group looking at her, admiring her. She looked wonderful today. Natural, interesting...and beautiful.

She wore jeans, slightly worn and perfectly fit to the lovely, firm curves of her hips and thighs. She had tried to tie her hair back from her face but, again, it fanned out into lovely silken curls around her high, flushed cheekbones. Her sweatshirt said *Writers are novel lovers*, and Mike found himself more than once distracted by the thought and wondering if it were true.

"Okay," Mike said finally, moving over to Mary's side. "Let's get the show on the road here." He bent down over the pile of equipment and picked up a bat. Then, with great theatrical fanfare, he swung it several times. The group laughed.

Polly explained, "Mike's our resident show-off, Mary. Don't believe any of it. He'll strike out just like the rest of them."

"Actually, love," Stu said, massaging Polly's neck, "give Gibs his due. Our token southpaw here can pitch a mighty fast ball."

"A relative term," shouted Jack Adams, a physics professor.

"Enough about me," Mike said. "You guys are just stalling, afraid to face defeat."

"In your dreams, Gibs," Jack yelled.

"It's going to rain, you know," Polly said sweetly.

"No!" a group of male voices shouted in unison and the group moved as a whole, as if directed by some unseen Casey Stengel, slipping on gloves, slapping backs and joking with a camaraderie that Mary found strangely exhilarating. She had never been a part of a group like this, never thought she wanted to be. She had been wrong.

"Listen you guys," Polly said, straightening her five-foot-three frame into a commanding position. "Let's make this males-versus-females, add some spice to the game."

Raucous male laughter greeted her proposal.

"I mean it. I suspect raw talent in Mike's protégée here, and it's been obvious for months that the women in this group are holding back so you guys don't feel threatened. It's time to shake you up."

Before the men knew what was happening, Polly had not only wheedled agreement out of them but had convinced them it was only fair that the men bat left-handed.

"Okay, it's settled. Come on, Mary," Polly Tolliver said, taking her by the arm and handing her a glove. "I don't know why Mike has been hiding you from us these weeks, but it's about time he shared you. Outta here, Gibs," she tossed back over her shoulder to Mike. "Mary and I are playing outfield where we can talk. None of you turkeys can hit that far anyway."

The two women linked arms and walked out across the dewy field. Above them the sun slipped down behind a bank of mottled gray clouds.

Polly glanced up at it. "I told 'em, but no one would listen. Men!" And then she laughed, a lighter version of her husband's chuckle, and Mary joined in as they found their spots in the outfield.

"This is a hodgepodge of people, isn't it," Mary mused. "I thought at first it would be the maintenance-department team." The players in the distance were in a heated argument over batting order.

"Maintenance department?" Polly said, and then she understood. "Oh, that. You mean because Mike is working there now."

Mary nodded.

Polly shook her head. "No, this group has known each other forever. I don't think Mike knows too many of the fellows he works with. And besides, that's only temporary."

"Temporary?" Mary spaced herself a little way from Polly but close enough so they could still talk. "Mike talks as if everything is temporary. But I thought he had a permanent job there. I'm not sure what you mean—"

Polly looked over at her and wrinkled her brow. Then she laughed. "Sure, sure you do," she said. "I mean that Mike's only working there because he wanted to get some things together in his head, kind of like a sabbatical, only Mike wanted—no, *needed*—to be doing something. Maintenance was perfect. He could work with his hands. Get to know every inch of campus. But next semester—at least if Bill Carroll, the president, and Stu get their way—Mike will be a professor in the business department."

Business department? Getting his head together? Mary was confused. Polly must be talking about the divorce, she decided, but she didn't have the feeling Mike was still grieving the loss of his marriage, at all. In fact, he seemed more together than most people she knew. *But why would he be working as a maintenance worker and then—*

The ball came out of nowhere, propelled through the sky like a comet. Mary heard yelling, cheering, loud, shrieking voices from beyond.

"Home run!" someone shouted.

"It's all yours, Mary," Polly said. She was bent over, her hands on her knees and her eyes bright as she watched Mary.

Mary gulped and squinted up at the sky. Then, more out of an instinct to protect herself than from anything else, Mary lifted her gloved hand. In the next instant she felt the sharp impact of the ball, felt the automatic curling of her fingers around the sphere, and then heard the exhilarated shriek of Polly Tolliver's voice. She stared at her hand. Then she looked at Polly. And then, with a shriek that caused several students to glance out of the library windows, Mary leaped wildly into the air.

From behind home plate, his hands on his hips and his head moving slowly from side to side, Mike watched her. "Well, I'll be damned," he said.

"She's a pro!" Stu shouted. "You brought a pro out here, Gibs. That's sabotage!"

"I swear I didn't—" And then he was laughing, watching the shell of Mary's usual constraint melt away into nothing. She was a kid, a spontaneous, ecstatic girl jumping into the air. Polly was hugging Mary now, and even from a distance Mike could see the dancing pin-points of gold light in Mary's eyes, the moist flush spreading across her cheeks, the joy of fun on her face.

The women cheered noisily and then the third player was up and a woman named Josie, who turned out to be a holy terror of a pitcher, struck him out.

The women were up to bat next and Josie turned out to be even more wicked with a bat than a ball. Polly was up next and surprised the men who crowded in as far as they could by popping it right over their heads and then sliding delightfully into second base. Mary hit a little dribble of a ball that Stu overthrew and by the end of the first inning the men were down three to zip.

"Okay," Stu counseled his teammates, "they were lucky and we were compassionate. But the time has come for—"

"War!" the men shouted in unison, waving their fists in the air.

But after three more ragged innings the women had picked up two more and the men had one measly run. Mike and Mary passed in crossing, as the teams switched places on the field. Her laughter floated all around her and he caught her as she ran, stopping her in midair. "You're a fake, Shields," he said as he looked up at her and spun her around. The sun had come out and haloed her head and at that moment Mike knew he had never seen a more beautiful sight.

"Fake, nothing, *Gibs*. It's called unleashed potential. And you're responsible!" Her eyes teased and he loved the carefree joy in her face. So much of Mary was planned and cautious and careful. But today there was none of that. She was like a bird set free on a hilltop.

And then she planted a quick kiss on his forehead and wriggled out of his embrace. "Got to go, Gibson. Team needs me and this hanky-panky is distracting."

He laughed, planted his Yankees hat on her head and watched her fly off.

"Hey, gals, this is only a game, you know." It was Jack from the physics department. "Lighten up a little!" he added.

"You mean lighten up and let you win?" Madge, his girlfriend shouted back. "Get real!" And they all took huge swigs of water from the plastic bottles on the bench and ran to their positions for another go-at-it.

"Even the sun came out to watch us win," Polly said as she squinted up at the sky, and then they settled down to another round of fierce play. At the end of two more innings the men conceded—claiming that it had nothing to do with the score but that the women looked awfully tired.

"Ha!" Mary laughed. "Look at them, Polly, all sweat and tears."

Mike came up and wrapped an arm around her. "Last time I take you anywhere, darlin'. You've ruined my reputation."

"Don't blame it on Mary, Gibs," one of the men yelled. "That happened a lo-o-o-o-ong time ago!" In the midst or the laughter and good-natured ribbing they managed to get the equipment tossed into three huge net bags to be lugged off to car trunks.

"Okay, gang," Stu said over the noise. "Everyone's invited to our house for food and beer. Winners get KP!"

The group rapidly scattered and Mike smiled down at Mary. "Want to go to the Tollivers'?"

"Of course!" she said. "But first I need a drink of water."

Mike nodded toward the library. "Okay. In there—"

Mary entered the dark marble lobby first and spotted the water fountain on the opposite wall. The half circle of wooden benches in the center were empty and she skirted them as she glided across the room.

A second later she heard the crash. She spun around just as Mike tumbled to the marble floor.

"Mike!" she screamed and was at his side in an instant. Several students stopped, but Mike waved them on. "I'm fine," he mumbled. "Damn stupid thing to do, but I'm fine."

He lifted himself easily from the floor, and Mary breathed a sigh of relief. "What happened?"

Mike looked behind him at the heavy wooden bench, then faced Mary with a lopsided grin. "Damn thing lurched right out in front of me."

"Mike—"

He shrugged, "Truth is, I didn't see it."

"Didn't see the bench?" Mary frowned. "Mike, it's as big as an elephant. What were you looking at?"

"Nothing." He turned, then, and glanced outside. The sun had come out from behind the clouds in the final innings of the game and had flooded the day with brief white sunshine. "It was too bright out there, too dark in here. For a minute I couldn't see," he said. And then he grinned again and leaned his head to one side, his eyes teasing Mary to make an issue of it. "Not a big deal, darlin'. Happens to all of us."

Mary frowned. It hadn't happened to her. The bench looked huge now, as she looked at it.

"I guess it was the ignominy of defeat," Mike was whispering in her ear. "It brought me to my knees, just like you do," and he left her laughing as he had hoped he would.

By the time they got to the Tollivers' rambling white house on the edge of campus the bench was forgotten, the sun had retreated for good and it was pouring rain.

Mike tucked Mary into his side and they ran, arms wrapped around each other, up to the house.

"I told you it would rain," Polly said at the door. She pulled them into the house and handed each of them a towel. "The sun just stuck around long enough to shine on *us,* right, Mary?" She grinned then and made a sweeping movement with one hand. "Make yourself at home. What you don't see, find or ask for or send Mike for it—he knows his way around. It's a help-yourself kind of place we run here."

The party was in full swing. Polly had filled baskets with chips and crackers, someone was stirring a huge pot of chili on the stove in the kitchen, and the smell of homemade bread wafted through the spacious, comfortable rooms. Mike grabbed them each a beer and then drew Mary back into the entrance hall and watched her while she fluffed her hair dry. Her cheeks were flushed and her hair was a mass of damp, lustrous black waves.

"There're a couple of someones I want you to meet," he said when she finished, and then he led her to the other end of the hall and looked up the curving oak staircase. Mary followed his gaze. Sitting at the top, their knees bent and their faces pushed against the stair rail, were two tow-headed children about six years old. "How're my buddies?" Mike called up.

The two youngsters broke into enormous grins that filled their entire faces. The little girl had Polly's round face, sparkling eyes and a sprinkling of freckles across her small nose. Her brother was a carbon copy, but with Stu's sharp intelligence and slight frown.

They came down the stairs in a single rush, tackling Mike at the bottom in a well-executed joint effort. He sat on the bottom step and pulled them down beside him.

"Okay guys, you win. Now I want you to meet a friend. Mary, this is Petey and Tizzy Tolliver—"

"No, Uncle Mike! I'm Liz," the little girl said, her scowl scolding Mike but her eyes sparkling.

"Yeah, that's it. These ragamuffins are *Lizzy* and Peter, the famous Tolliver twins," Mike said, hugging both of the kids. "Kids, this is my friend Mary."

"Hi," they each said, suddenly shy. They looked up at her, appraising her innocently.

Mary was taken aback for a minute—not at the children but at the picture that was presented in front of her. It was such a family shot, Mike and these beautiful kids, and they were as crazy about Mike as he was about them. It shouldn't have been a surprise, she supposed. Mike had shown the same easiness with his nieces and nephews. But that had been family, an expected sort of thing. Somehow it was different tonight, watching this strong, virile person bending and playing and laughing with an abandon that matched the two children huddled beside him. "Hi, Lizzy and Peter," Mary said.

"I lost a tooth," Lizzy said proudly, proving it with a grin.

"Good grief," Mike said in supposed shock. "Well, come on, let's find it!"

"Uncle Mike's kinda silly," Liz explained patiently, and Mary nodded as she and Lizzy shared an instant female understanding.

"Well, what have we here?" Polly appeared carrying a tray of hot nachos.

"Nachos!" the twins said in unison, and Polly shooed them off to the kitchen to make themselves a small platter that they could eat upstairs before they brushed their teeth and hopped into bed.

"Polly, what beautiful children you have."

"Yes," she said, her eyes sparkling. "They are that. And they are also spoiled rotten, especially since Mike came back home."

"Polly's been a little miffed ever since Stu and I took the twins on a canoe trip without her."

"Now that's a blooming lie as long as your nose, Gibs. *Never* would I begrudge you and Stu the treat of living in a drafty tent with two children and two thousand mosquitoes."

Mary laughed.

"Hey, Uncle Mike—" It was Pete, his blond head sticking through the door. "Is it true...about the game...?"

"Hey, you know how it is with girls, Petey. Sometimes you just have to—"

But Mary and Polly had muzzled Mike with their hands before he could speak any more and then they all laughed, including Pete.

"Chili is ready!" someone hollered from the kitchen and Polly went scurrying off to pull out soup bowls.

Mary watched her hurry off. "You like kids, don't you."

"These two are special. Like my own."

"Will you have your own?"

"Sure, I hope so. I'll need help, but considering all things, I'd love to have kids."

Mary nodded. She had never thought much about it, probably because she was an only child. Growing up to be a mother was never uppermost in her mind. She could not even remember playing house as a child. But seeing this family, the feeling that surrounded them, made her wonder. Maybe someday, after a few other lives were lived... Aloud she said, "I really like your friends, Mike. After three hours, I feel as if I've known them all my life."

"Yeah, they're like that. I like them, too. And I like Polly's chili almost as much. We better make our move before it disappears."

Much later, after the soup pot was scrubbed and put away and the last crumb of apple pie had been stolen from the tin, Mary and Mike finally pulled themselves out of the large, comfortable chairs in the living room and looked out at the rain. It was coming down in silver sheets now, pelting relentlessly against the windowpanes.

"You're welcome to stay until it lets up," Polly offered.

Mike glanced over at Stu. His head was resting against the cushions of a recliner chair and his eyes were peacefully closed. He laughed. "Stu's energy wears me out, Pol. I think we'd better be off."

"Well, at least take this umbrella. It's the only one left—"

She pushed the umbrella into their hands and after a rush of thanks and "we'll-do-it-again-soon's," Mary and Mike hurried off into the dark night. The rain, whipped up beneath the umbrella by the wind, pummeled their shoulders and made them run faster, laughing into the wet night.

"Even this downpour can't dampen the day, Mike," Mary said when they reached her house. "It was absolutely lovely, one of the best I've had."

Mike partly turned in the seat to face her. A sliver of light from the street lamp fell across Mary's face, highlighting the day's glow. He reached out and touched it. "Don't ever again tell me you don't play ball."

Mary grinned. "With you, Mike, I'll play ball anytime." She took his hand and held it there against her cheek, her eyes half closed. "I'm utterly exhausted, and more alive than I've been in a long time. Funny, isn't it? You are a wonderful tonic for me, Michael Gibson."

They were friends, comfortable, easy friends, but the undertow rose up now at the slightest provocation, rushed up and grabbed at Mike, twisted his insides painfully. He watched the expressions flit across her face; saw there the mirror of his desire, and he gently pulled his hand away. "Come on, let's get you inside."

Mary went willingly, ducking beneath the proffered umbrella and wrapping her arm around Mike's waist, hurrying along beside him as they made their way to the door.

But once they reached it, Mike turned toward her, kissed her somberly and was gone, lost in the silvery sheets of rain.

WHEN THE PHONE CALL CAME, Michael was still awake, wondering about the woman who had inched her way into his heart. He couldn't shake her off, couldn't satisfy himself with the significant friendship they had begun. The day replayed itself in his mind, but the scenes that lingered, frozen in still frames, were those of Mary—Mary swept up in his arms on the ball field, Mary laughing uproariously when she caught the ball, Mary looking up at him with eyes that spoke volumes—and had thrown him into complete chaos.

He reached for the phone in the dark and mumbled a hello.

The voice at the other end was high-pitched, excited, and at first he didn't recognize it. Finally the words registered.

"Michael," she said, "Michael can you come? It's my house...the cottage...the basement...it's drowning!"

Chapter Nine

He threw on an old shirt, pulled on a pair of jeans and was out of the house before the phone line was cold.

Mary's message had been muddled, but the only thing that mattered was clear: she needed him.

The car clock said 3:00 a.m. and Michael half smiled at the irony of it. Some people had their own songs; maybe he and Mary were developing their own hour. And if she wanted to pick one, the middle of the night was fine with him. He drove on, through the deepening puddles along the sides of the road, and on toward campus.

Mary was waiting at the door but he could barely see her. Between them was a screen of pelting rain.

"Okay," he said when he was finally inside, "lead the way, damsel in distress." He had left in a rush, without a jacket or raincoat, and was already drenched to the skin. He reached up and touched her cheek. It was pale now, empty of the glow he had left her with earlier. "You okay?"

She smiled. "Now I am."

They walked to the top of the basement stairs and Mike flicked on the flashlight he had taken out of his toolbox. The beam traveled down the narrow stairway until it began to weave in distorted patterns as the light fell onto a moving mass of water. "Looks like the mighty Mississippi has arrived."

"Yes," she murmured behind him, her eyes searching into the dark cave below. "And me without my riverboat."

Mike started down the steps with Mary close behind. She was wearing thin flannel pajamas and Michael could feel every small curve of her body as she bumped against his back.

"Did you have anything down here?" he asked.

"Some books, but I was able to rescue most of them. And there's a trunk somewhere—"

"It's a good thing you woke up."

"I...I hadn't gone to sleep. I came down here to look for a book. That's when I discovered it."

"There—look there." The beam of the flashlight stopped at a window well close to the ceiling. Pouring down the rough concrete walls from a gash in the window was a torrent of water. It had flooded the entire basement floor and water was easing its way up the stairs, sloshing gently against the steps. "I think I can block it best from the outside, then we'll figure out why the drain isn't working."

Mike was back up the stairs and outside in no time, taking with him a pile of towels Mary found in a cabinet. With his flashlight wedged between two rocks, he managed to find the broken window, pad it with rags and then, with the aid of several sandbags from his trunk, he blocked off the water flowing down into the well. A tight crash of thunder followed him into the house.

When he got back inside, Mary was down in the basement, her pajama legs rolled up to her knees. With the wavering light from a lantern balanced on the middle step, she was feeling her way toward the drain.

"Mary, come out of that mess," Mike called from the stairs.

She looked up at Michael. The light was beneath him, shining up toward his face. Her smile grew. "Michael, I wish you could see yourself."

Michael looked down at the thin, transparent shirt plastered against his chest. Rainwater ran down his face and fell from his chin in tiny rivulets. And then they both laughed, caught up in the ludicrousness of the situation, and Michael pulled off his soggy tennis shoes, hiked up his jeans and joined her in the murky waters of the basement.

"I hope there isn't anything down here I don't want to know about," she said, rolling her sleeves up above her elbows. "Gads, what a mess!"

Mike shoved his wet, dripping hair back from his face. "That's putting it mildly." He pushed his feet along the slanting floor, searching for the drain. "Why were you still awake?"

"I was waiting for three o'clock to roll around, so I could call you."

"Of course. I should have known that."

"Yes—"

"I think . . . yes. Voilà!" Mike shouted.

Mary jumped. "What?"

"The drain, sorry. I didn't mean to scare you. Here, hold the light, okay?"

Mary took the flashlight and aimed it down toward the water. Mike bent over and groped around, his hands sliding along the floor. There it was, a mass of debris collected in the sloping area. As soon as Mike dug it out with his fingers, a miniature whirlpool spun down the pipes. "Is this the book you were looking for?" Mike held up a soggy, limp volume that had been wedged in with the debris.

Mary directed the beam of light to the cover. "*Home Maintenance Repairs*," she read, and then they both began to laugh, relieved, weary laughter that swirled around the dank basement. Their eerie shadows danced along the walls.

"What do you say we get out of here?" Mary suggested.

"Oh, I don't know, there's a certain charm, a certain ambience down here—" He did a shuffling two-step that sent water splashing about between them.

"Gibson, up! I'm freezing—" Mary gave him a playful shove, then scooted beyond him and sloshed up the stairs.

Mike followed.

When they reached the top and moved into the light of Mary's hallway, she looked at Mike in dismay. "Oh, Mike," she said, "you're absolutely soaked!"

"Absolutely. It's raining out," he said with a half smile. His shirt was drenched all the way through; his jeans, a heavy coat of denim plastered against his legs. His feet were bare.

"You'll catch pneumonia! The air has turned bitter, Mike. You can't go home like that."

"I guess I could borrow your jeans." His eyes were full of laughter.

"No, no. I'll tell you what you'll do. You go in there—" she pointed down the hall toward the bath-room, "and I'll dry your clothes while you shower. There's a big old robe in there that will fit you in the meantime. You're soaked all the way through to the bone. Your hair—"

She reached up and touched his hair then, and a sudden soft shock washed through Michael. He looked down at her. Had she felt it, too? She must have. She *did,* it was clear, now, obvious in the slight curve of her lips, but even more in the dancing light in her eyes and the slightly ragged breath she took before dropping her hand.

Mary's fingers were hot where they had touched him, as hot and tingling as if she had touched a live wire. Overhead, the storm was bumping and rumbling sullenly against the roof. She managed a tight smile, a look up into his eyes. "Well, go on now..." and she turned slowly, and headed for the kitchen to start a pot of coffee.

Michael dumped his clothes outside the bathroom door and stepped into the shower. Being in Mary's bathroom did not help soothe the sensations that were creating havoc inside of him. The room was filled with the clean, soapy smell of her. It was everywhere, clinging to the tile, floating about on the hot, steamy air. Or maybe it was inside him, permanently etched there now. He scrubbed his body vigorously, blocking out thought and giving vent to the enormous buildup of emotion inside of him. For days he had held himself back, avoided what he knew now was going to happen.

He and Mary were going to make love together. Gently and lovingly and with all the gathered feelings that had been growing like wildflowers inside of him. And he knew it was not wise, he knew it would lead to things that would be difficult to handle, and he knew it was too late to do a damn thing about it.

When he finished he tied the robe around him and walked out to the softly lit living room. She had started a fire on the small hearth and was sitting in front of it on the couch, her knees pulled up to her chin, a dry robe tucked around her. On the coffee table was a pot of coffee, cups and cream, a bottle of wine, liqueurs and several glasses.

"Are we having a party?" he asked, taking in the scene.

Mary looked up. Her hair was still damp and it glistened in the firelight when she shook her head. "I wasn't sure what you wanted. I didn't know what would warm you better—coffee or wine."

He walked over and sat down beside her. "Do you really want to know what would warm me?"

"A bit of each," she said quickly, pouring him a cup of coffee. Her hand shook slightly and she stopped, then set the pot down. "I . . . Michael, I . . ."

In the distance he could hear the rhythmic slap of his clothes against the sides of the dryer. Farther away, there was the sound of thunder, a low, rolling crash that drowned out Mary's voice.

Michael poured two glasses of wine, then smiled at her. "There, now it's all set, a spread to match every taste. The fire feels nice. That was a good idea."

"It's freezing," she said. Her body shivered slightly.

"Here, this'll help." He took a small throw from the back of the couch and slipped it over her shoulders, then handed her a glass of wine. One hand lingered beneath her hair, lightly touching the soft skin on the back of her neck.

"I'm sorry for dragging you over here."

"You'd only have to be sorry if I resented it, or if you resented my coming, or if we made a mess of things."

"It was something to say—"

"I know."

"You've been such a good friend, Michael," she began.

"What's with this past-tense stuff, darlin'? I don't take my friendships lightly. We'll always be friends, no matter—"

"Maybe, but—"

"No maybes, no buts—"

A high, abrupt clap clipped off his words. The room shimmered suddenly in the flash of lightning. There was a popping noise in the distance and then the small lamp light disappeared, the lights in the kitchen flickered and went out and the house was left in darkness save for the dancing shadows created by the firelight.

"A transformer blew," Mike said. "There isn't anything we can do about it."

"I found a cache of candles in the cabinet, just in case something happened." She pointed toward the end table where she had lined them up, a half dozen fat colored candles.

"So that's it. You planned all this—"

"Absolutely." She sipped her wine and watched him over the rim of the glass. The darkness and warmth of the fire seeped into her and she felt both safety and courage in the shadowy night. "I planned the whole thing, the basement flood at three in the morning, the lightning, the rain. I'm a brazen hussy at heart."

"I can see that," Mike said, his fingers playing with her hair.

She smiled then, dreamily, and looked deep into the fire. "I *have* been that way, you know. I've been brazen, I've been docile, I've been intelligent and witty and outgoing. Exotic and sexy and alluring. I invented the me that was all those things at one time or another."

"By writing about them."

"Yes. That's why I started writing. It began innocently enough—I had nothing else to do." She half smiled at him, then looked back into the fire and went on. "My one best friend from high school had gone off to Duke University—I was supposed to have gone with her, but then my father got sick. Tanya would write me these wonderful letters from school about the incredible life she was living. She'd talk about tangling with new ideas—about people she had met who were opening up her mind to worlds she and I had never dreamed about. She talked about men, about losing her virginity to a student from France who took her to a huge beach house he rented. He lit candles all over the house, played Beethoven on the stereo and made mad, passionate love to her until the sun came up over the ocean.

"I wrote her back, but it was always so hard. My life was the same she knew about, that same one that had held her until she broke free. There was me and my father and the ladies bringing pies. I had some courses at the community college, but even that was empty compared to what Tanya was living. So I started picking out little things that happened to me, tiny incidences from class, or things about people who came to visit my father, or even strangers I'd watch in restaurants. And I'd imagine myself with these people, interacting with them, running off with some of them to far-flung corners of the earth. Living wildly and recklessly.''

"And you wrote about all that to Tanya."

She laughed. "Yes. At first I did. But then they got too unbelievable, and I didn't want my stories disturbed by someone scrutinizing their veracity, so I kept on writing them, but only in loose-leaf binders that I kept in my bedroom closet.''

"Did you ever show your father?"

"No." Her answer was short, clipped. "I showed my father the things I wrote for class, though. At least some of them. I showed them to him after the teachers had written their wonderful, encouraging comments all over them. I let him see my *A*'s and *A pluses* and the short notes that said, 'You have real talent, Mary Elizabeth.'"

"He must have been proud of you."

"He never said," she said slowly. "Teachers' comments were never very important to my father."

"He'd certainly be proud of you now."

Mary shook her head, slowly, almost in slow-motion. She looked over at Mike and absently rubbed the back of her hand against her cheek, a childlike gesture that touched him. And then she said softly, "Well, he would or he wouldn't. It doesn't matter. There. Now I've told you that."

She picked up her glass and began to sip the wine slowly, peacefully, as if she had brought relief to herself by telling him that story. At times like this Mary's vulnerability was so acute it almost hurt Mike to watch it.

He slipped his arm around her shoulders and pulled her close. A drop of wine spilled down onto her fingers. Mike dipped his head and began to lick it off.

Mary shivered but did not pull away. The need had been rising in her for days, like the storm, a slow, gentle buildup that was bound—that *had*—to eventually erupt and explode its power.

She wanted Mike, and she wasn't afraid. Whatever it was she felt had a rightness about it that she had never felt about a man before. Not anyone. Mike's tongue on her fingers was hot and lazy and filled her with such delight she moaned softly into the curve of his neck. And then she pressed into him, her body curved to his like a spanned bow.

"Mike, I . . . I don't do this easily—"

He brought his head up. "I know, darlin', I know that."

"I mean, it's you, you started out as a friend, a *safe*, funny, gentle friend."

She gazed at him, as if something momentous lay in her words, in his response to them.

He half smiled. "I'm still safe, Mary. Still a friend." He threaded his fingers through her hair and held her there, gazing into the deep emerald pools of her eyes. There were dancing lights and flickers of gold, but there was something else that gripped his soul: a fierce, raw desire that shook him, even as it swept him with delight.

He started to speak, checked himself and drew her close to him, cradling her head against his chest. A new wave of desire swept through him with astonishing force. What power there is in all this, he thought to himself. Staggering, overwhelming power. "So, rain tree man," she murmured against his jaw. "What do you think?"

"Think..." He smiled down at her. "I have to do that, too?"

"We can skip it, I guess." She shifted until the tip of her tongue touched his lips. With slow, languorous movement, she traced the outline of his mouth.

Mike breathed in broken, panting phrases. "I know..." he said, "this...must be the hussy speaking."

She caught his lip between her teeth and nibbled lightly.

Mike's hands slid between the folds of her robe, down her fine electric body. "Oh, Mary," he moaned, "I want you, darlin'. I want you, now."

There was no hesitancy, no slight pulling back. She answered him with her quick, suppliant tongue.

"Then, I think we shall," she said, at last, her voice barely audible beneath the drumming of their hearts.

THE EMBERS WERE LOW, casting an eerie glow across the room, when Mike awoke. They had tossed a thick rug in front of the fire many hours before and Mary was curled up beside him on it now, one arm flung haphazardly across his chest. A plump down comforter covered their naked bodies.

Mike slowly eased himself out from beneath her arm and the blanket, then moved to the fire and stoked new life into it.

He threw on a few more logs and in minutes was back beside her, down beneath the blanket and feeling the soothing beat of her heart and the warmth of her blood as it moved through her body. He held her more tenderly, he thought, than a man had ever held a woman. She was even more beautiful than he had imagined, her whole body an artist's smooth, lovely blend of light and shadow, curve and plane. Their lovemaking had matched the rhythm of the fire's dance, a true, tumultuous union that he could not have imagined.

Mary hadn't held back, hadn't been shy as he half expected, but instead she had met him desire for desire, cadence for cadence, until they burst forth together, pleasing and giving and loving each other again and again. She was an exotic seabird, flying off and coming back to him, lighting and lifting, filling him with all the incredible delight he had denied himself for such a long time.

Finally, exhausted, they had fallen back in one another's arms and drifted into a deep, dreamless sleep.

Michael traced his finger along the contour of her breast with the familiarity born of their lovemaking. He lowered his head then and kissed it lightly.

Mary stirred. Slowly, blissfully, she pulled her lids open.

"Hi," he said.

"Hi, yourself." Her voice came from deep in her throat, a sleepy, husky sound. Across her forehead a lock of black wavy hair fell lazily. But it was her smile that did Mike in, that lazy, sexy smile, saturated with the delight of the hours before.

His finger continued mapping trails across, around, beneath her breasts. "So," he said, his eyes not leaving her face, "now what?"

Her eyes were calm and as green as the sea. "What are the choices?" she asked.

"I could make you breakfast—" He rubbed his palm across the flat plane of her tummy.

"Breakfast . . ." Mary brought one finger up to his chest. "Or?" she urged him on.

"Or we could go out for breakfast."

She smiled. "Yes, we could. Or—"

"Or we could read—poetry, cartoons, *War and Peace.*" He bent low, then, rubbing his cheek against her breast, and soon his tongue began blazing a slow, tantalizing circle.

Mary stirred. The familiar inner fires began their gentle licking, teasing her, lifting her, and then swiftly the fires grew and a rush of desire so strong she thought she might explode blanketed her whole being.

"Oh, Mike," she moaned, her back arching against the thick rug.

"And yes," he said raggedly, "there's always that. We could do that, too."

He lifted himself on his elbow and then with great ease, he slipped over her amazing body and into her, certain that no man and woman had ever before experienced such great delight.

And as he loved her in the bright light of the new day, it all fell away: the careful plans, the goals, the intense ordering of his life. The great, gray weight was gone, and for that lovely instant, there was not any time at all, only the infinite joy of their loving.

BREAKFAST WAS MUCH LATER, a lazy, middle-of-the-day Sunday breakfast of eggs and bacon and mugs filled with strong, hot coffee.

Food had never tasted this good to Mary. "You're a drug, Michael," she said, pushing her chair back and lifting her feet to rest in his lap. Mike gently rubbed the soles of her bare feet. "That's because I am such an incredible cook."

"No, it's because you're such an incredible lover."

"You think so, do you?"

"I do. Yes, I certainly do. You are that, and more."

Michael could see the change in Mary. There was a glowing, soaring sensation inside himself that was undeniable, but in Mary it was so visible he thought he could reach out and touch it. She was blushing, loose, as alive as a forest creature after a spring rain. Her luminous eyes had deepened to an exquisite sea green and there was a hidden music in the way she moved, the way she spoke.

"You're staring at me, Michael," she said softly.

"*Gazing,* not staring. Gazing in absolute delight." Reluctantly, he slipped her feet from his lap and stood. "And I'd like to go on doing it all day. All day long—" He bent and dropped small kisses along the crest of her hair. "But I can't, Mary. I need to go."

"Go?" Mary started. What did she think? That he would spend the day, the night, move in with her? Of course not! But the thought of him leaving so soon brought a cool breeze into their lovely cocoon. She swallowed the feeling and stood, then smiled up at him. "Of course you do. As lovely as it sounds, I know I can't keep you wrapped up here with me, shamelessly making love on my living-room floor—"

"Hm-m-m, well you *could,* I mean, if you really wanted to—" He tipped his head to one side and looked down at her. "You really shouldn't say things like that to me, you know. It does strange things to my insides . . . and my outsides. What are people going to think?"

Mary smiled back. "Good. Wherever you're going, I want everyone to know, to look at you and say, 'Aha, *I* know what that man has been doing—'"

He drew her into the circle of his arms and kissed her. "That's fine with me. The whole world can know, for all I care."

Mary stayed close in his arms. "Do you have to work today?"

"Nope. President Carroll wants to see me."

"On Sunday?"

"He's leaving town for a few days. Today was the best we could do."

With the palms of her hands flat on his chest, she looked up into his eyes. She spoke carefully, not wanting to put claims on him. "Mike, I've tried to figure you out. You tell me bits and pieces about yourself, but somehow they never add up to a whole."

Mike frowned.

"About your job, I mean."

Her eyes searched his.

Things were different today, no matter how Mike wanted it to be or what he thought; they were simply changed. Mary Shields was special, special in his life, a special relationship, and last night confirmed it. He knew it couldn't go anywhere, not beyond the boundaries of Chestershire and Mary's short time at the college, but for now it was very real.

"Sometimes I feel," Mary was saying beside him, "that your life is a series of neat compartments, like rooms, and you pick and choose who will come into which room. I mean all this stuff about working as a maintenance man, the degree from Harvard, and then hearing from Polly that Stu is trying to get you to teach in his department. I...I don't mean to sound possessive or grasping, Mike—those are rights I don't have and I don't even want them—I only want to know you."

Her last sentence ended on such a soft breath of emotion that Mike had to listen hard to hear her. He looked down at her and felt his heart constrict. *Oh, Mary,* he thought, *you're so special, and that's the problem, don't you see?* But he didn't speak his thoughts. Instead he leaned his head to one side and looked into her eyes. "Mary, you're right. I've given you half answers, even when I knew it confused you. I've been kind of a dope about this, haven't I?"

"Yes," she said simply and they both laughed.

"I guess in the beginning I liked getting to know you as what I am right now—Mike the maintenance man. And it seemed to make *you* comfortable, too. I think in your mind it was easier to let a handyman befriend you than, say, a professor of art, an English professor, college administrator, what have you. There was less chance, maybe, of that kind of friendship being any more than a friendship." He searched her eyes for affirmation of his words.

She half smiled. "I...well, maybe. A handyman for a friend has a kind of built-in safety net about it, I guess. It's silly, isn't it? You're you, no matter what your job, what you do. And, yet you're right. I felt safe with that Mike."

He tipped her chin up so he could look down into those beautiful eyes. "I wasn't trying to deceive you. It simply didn't seem to need an explanation at first. I mean we were strangers sharing a dryer."

"We still are—sharing a dryer, I mean."

Mike laughed and steeled himself, because her light laughter was releasing the demon again, and if he didn't watch himself, Bill Carroll was going to be meeting with an empty chair.

"Yes," he said, swallowing the lump. "Well, anyway, I *like* being a handyman here. I wanted to do this. When I left California and came back home, I had some things to work out. I needed some time to give my mind a rest. But I'm not the type to sit around, even while taking a break. This seemed the perfect interim solution, and after some mighty fancy arguing I talked Bill Carroll into it. This job has given me a chance to do some things I haven't had time to do for years."

"Fix drains and squeaky doors?"

"Don't be flip, Mary, or I'll have to think of a way to silence you—" He brushed her hair back from her face. She was truly beautiful. Why hadn't he seen that before? Had he? "No," he said, "squeaky doors aren't a career goal for me, but the time, the space, working with my hands, being on campus, those were all good things."

"So now you're all together, you've gotten over your divorce—"

"—gotten over my divorce?"

"Well, I just assumed . . . I mean, I thought maybe that was why you needed the breathing time."

Mike played with the hair at the base of her neck. He laughed shortly. "I . . . no. I've been divorced for several years, Mary, and it wasn't that hard to get over. It was all very amicable, as they say."

"Oh." Mary looked down at the swirly pattern in the linoleum floor.

"Well, anyway, back to the point at hand, it looks like I'm going to move into academia next year, and I can only hope—" He kissed the top of her head, "that it won't put too severe a strain on our friendship. Beneath my patched corduroy jacket and horn-rimmed glasses, I'll still be Mike the handyman at heart."

Mary lifted her head again. She found it hard to refrain from looking at him for very long, from being in touch with the midnight blue eyes that made her feel connected, in touch. And suddenly the thought that she would not be around when Mike moved into his new job entered her mind, and then her heart. And it brought with it a sudden jolt of surprising pain.

When Mike walked out the door a short while later, he was humming. The day had brightened with a vengeance, pushing yesterday's wind and rain into far-off memory. Mike could feel the brightness, the energy, as he strolled down the walk. And then, as he moved out of the shadows of Mary's cottage, the brilliance of the cold sunlight hit him fully and he squinted into the light. He stopped for a moment, remembering his stumble of the day before, his need to call the doctor in Indianapolis soon, but mostly remembering the uncomfortable truth that he still hadn't let Mary into all the rooms.

Chapter Ten

The world had changed. When she ventured out into it after that night, everything was different. The colors of the day were brighter, brilliant oranges and reds and saffron yellows. The smells of fall were everywhere, the pungent odor of burning leaves and the earthy fragrance of thick wool sweaters just removed from storage. Even the sounds of her heart were different, brighter and quicker. She loved it all, each day, each change, each moment with Mike, and even those away from him, when she crawled inside her mind and relived the wonder of this man, who had brought such unexpected joy into her life. She hadn't expected it, hadn't looked for it, and there it was.

She refused to look at time, at the numbered days until she would have to leave Chestershire. It was not relevant, somehow; did not fit into this new, dazzling world. Somehow she knew it would work out, that the fullness inside of her, the happiness that filled her, could not evaporate. Somehow, some way, it would have to continue, because to think otherwise was contrary to everything she felt.

Her writing took on new passion, the difficult Nicholas's personality erupted like a burst of energy and the writer's workshop became a vibrant backdrop for the time spent with Mike.

A few days later Mary met Mike after work at Nick's, a favorite campus watering hole. He was there before her, his long legs wrapped around the bar stool and his laughing eyes charming Ruthie, the waitress. Her heart skipped a beat.

"Hi," she said, slipping onto the seat beside him. He looked at her for a long moment before he spoke, and Mary felt her blood heat up. He was the most unusual man she'd ever met. His eyes would glisten with overt sensuality, and yet running beneath it all, grounding it, was a great kindness. The combination turned her insides to melted butter. She touched his arm, smiled softly.

"Mary," he said, "you're truly beautiful." He leaned over and kissed the tip of her nose, then her forehead and the curve of her ear.

And "beautiful" to Mary, beneath Mike's gaze, took on meanings that far transcended the way she looked. "Mike," she breathed, "don't do that. I...I'll dissolve and then you'll be sitting here with a pool of something, quivering Jell-O or a puddle of honey or something. You do it to me, you know, those looks and touches and—"

"Sh-h-h." He kissed her again, stopping the rush of words that escaped her slightly parted lips.

"Well, now this is a fine kettle of fish," Ruthie said at Mike's elbow.

They pulled apart and Mary smiled sheepishly at the waitress.

"I thought Mike was saving himself for me," Ruthie said in her rough smoker's voice. "We made a deal— remember, Mike?"

Mike nodded, his face serious. "Of course, Ruth. If you saved my place in here I would marry you. You just tell me when."

"Liar," she laughed. "And who says I'd want you anyway?" She slapped his knee with a towel. "You watch yourself with this one, Mary. Can't trust him further than you can throw him, not one with those eyes."

Mary laughed and Mike bent over and gave Ruthie a hug, then whispered something in her ear that made her both grin and swat Mike again with her towel.

Mary watched Ruthie saunter off. When she looked back at Mike there was an intensity in her eyes that surprised him.

"Mary, what is it? Not Ruthie… Hey, we kid all the time."

She laughed, but it was a forced, small laugh. "No, it's not Ruthie. It's us, you and me and how wonderful all this is right now."

Her hands were resting on the bar and Mike traced wavy lines across them with his finger. He lifted one hand then and kissed the pads of her fingers. "You're funny, Mary, unpredictable sometimes. But, yes, you're right. Wonderful, it is," he said.

"And I just want you to know, I mean—"

Her eyes were bright, filled with energy and dancing flecks of gold. He found it hard to concentrate on what she was saying.

"Mike, listen, I just want the next few weeks, I mean, I don't expect anything from you—"

He leaned his head to one side. He frowned. "I'm not sure I understand—"

Suddenly her eyes filled with tears. "Oh, Mike, I don't know. I don't know what I'm trying to say. Except last night I lay awake thinking about the best time I had ever had in my life."

She took a deep breath. "It was the first summer when my friends returned from college. Our housekeeper, Haddie Sheehan, had concocted some story so my dad would let me go, and my friends and I, we went away for two weeks. One of the guy's parents owned a wonderful rustic cottage in Maine and it was all ours for those days—just the six of us. I was absolutely free for two whole weeks. We played and swam and climbed the rugged rocks that jutted out into the ocean. The sun turned my skin brown and my muscles grew hard from running along the sand and swimming against the waves. We ate lobster and corn while the sun sank down into the ocean and it was glorious, the very best time of my whole life. But now, these days, these weeks with you..." she said, and then her voice broke, stopped by a lump that formed suddenly in her throat. She swallowed hard.

When she spoke again her voice was gravely calm. "These days with you, Michael, are without measure. Whatever happens, let's not spoil them. Let's allow them to be, just as they are, a gift to each other, a—" She stopped and breathed deeply.

Mike tried to listen to her words, to understand what was coming out in this unexpected flow of emotion. He curved his fingers beneath her chin and tipped her head back, looked intently into the deep green sea of her eyes. "Mary," he said, smiling gently, "would you come home with me?"

"Now?"

"Now."

She took his hand and held it to her cheek for a minute. "Are you saying I talk too much?"

He grinned at her, then stood up and looked down at her. "Me? Say that? About you?"

Mary did not answer. Instead she slipped from the tall stool and walked quietly out of the bar with Mike at her side and her heart balancing on her arm, right out there for the whole world to see.

THE NEXT DAY, after Mary left, Mike scanned the mail that the housekeeper had left on the hall table the day before. There was one package, a small, overnight mail delivery, which he opened quickly. He pulled out a sheet of paper and scanned the note impatiently.

It was from his brother Andy. It read:

Mike,

I spoke with Doc Seaver about your stumble the other day and he prescribed these dark glasses. Wear them whenever you're in bright sunshine or when there's a glare. I think they're kind of sexy, whatta you say? He said there's no need to come in until your next appointment, but to call anytime if you have questions. I'll call soon, but I wanted to get these specs Fed-Exed pronto; hence the note. Talk to you soon.

Andy

P.S. A WRITER! Maybe there's hope for you yet. When do I get to meet this incredible bundle of literacy? I've received varying reports. Franny says she's friendly, Mom says she's lovely; Alex, the teenage hormone hazard, says she's hot, and Dad just smiles. What gives?

Mike pulled the glasses out of the package and stared at them. The lenses were dark, nearly black. Mike frowned. An image of Jack Nicholson danced crazily across his mind.

Then, his jaw tight and the lines in his forehead deepening, he threw the pair of sunglasses down on the table. They bounced once, then lay there flat and threatening.

Without another look at them, Mike walked out of the house and slammed the door fiercely behind himself.

IT WAS TWO DAYS LATER before he wore them, two frustrating days and one painful night. He'd been so damn controlled about it all. Why did a pair of sunglasses throw him so? Hell, everyone wore sunglasses.

He showed up at Mary's workshop building a few minutes before lunch. It was a crisp, bright autumn day. Mary bounded out of the building, the new lightness to her step bringing a grin to Mike's face, and then she stopped short halfway down the steps.

"Well?" he asked. The dark-rimmed sunglasses rested on his nose.

She wrinkled her forehead and brought one finger up to her cheek. "Macho," she said finally, then continued on toward him and linked her arm in his. "Definitely macho."

"Not sexy? My brother Andy thinks they're sexy."

Mary stopped walking and swung around in front of him, holding him still with her outstretched arms. "Sexy, hmmm." Her brows pulled together in strenuous thought.

Mike shrugged from her hold, pulled his shirt open, shifted his weight to one hip and lifted one shaggy brow. "Well?" he said in a husky baritone.

Mary burst into laughter, something she did so easily these days, and she leaned over and kissed the exposed bare slice of his chest. "Yeah, definitely sexy," she said when she pulled away. "Andy's right."

Mike pulled her into his side and they walked slowly over to the gazebo. It was shaded by two gigantic rain trees and had become their favorite spot to eat on pleasant days.

"Where'd you get the glasses?" Mary asked casually as Mike pulled out their sandwiches.

"My brother sent them."

"Sunglasses? Your brother sent you sunglasses?"

"They have a slight prescription. Andy's the one in med school studying to be an ophthalmologist."

"Oh," Mary said, "so it's like a perk."

"Something like that," Mike said. He folded his hands behind his head and watched her.

"Well, I like you in glasses. They make you look...oh, sexily sophisticated." She smoothed a napkin out on her lap and began to eat her sandwich.

Mike laughed and stretched his feet out in front of him. She was like a cool breeze that soothed him, washed over him and made the day bright and right again. He watched her obvious enjoyment in the sandwich he had brought. She licked a crumb from the corner of her mouth and the small movement did its damage, sending a slow, visceral rush of desire through him. Mike winced. In addition to all the other things, she had this zany power to turn him on in an instant, in the middle of the day, by eating a sandwich. Sophisticated? Hell, he was about as sophisticated these days as a hot-blooded eighteen-year-old.

"What?" she said, seeing the silly grin spread across his face.

"No 'what's.' Tell me something, Mary. How are you going to handle yourself back in New York after this life of being a kept woman. I mean, will you starve without someone to make you sandwiches every day?''

"I'm spoiled, aren't I?" she said happily.

"Absolutely."

"Maybe I'll have to take you with me."

Mike laughed.

"We could open up a little sandwich shop on a corner in the middle of Manhattan."

"No, it would have to be a cart, Mike's sandwich cart. Then I could move about, gather grist for the mill as I rub shoulders with mankind, feeding its hungry bodies and probing its tormented souls."

"Exactly! And after a long day's work we could—"

Mike lifted one brow. "Yes . . . ?"

"Well," she said slowly.

She spoke with a coyness that was new to her, a beguiling trait that had been spun from their lovemaking. It surprised and amused Michael. "Maybe," he said, "we'd better talk about the nights later."

Mary glanced at her watch. "Maybe you're right. No sense in leading a horse to water and not letting it drink."

"Mary!"

Mary stood and shook her head. "I was once a quiet, controlled, nice person. See, Michael Gibson, just see what you've done to me?"

He stood up beside her, looked down into the lovely sparkling laughter in her eyes. "I'd love to take the credit for it, but it was there all the time, Mary, just waiting for a few layers to be peeled off. Yep, it was,

I'm sure of it—'' His voice drifted off and he kissed her, slowly, lovingly, and then they parted and each walked away with it, with the tender joy of that single kiss.

MARY WAS NERVOUS. She had liked the Tollivers immediately; the day they had all spent together playing ball and eating chili had been great, relaxed fun.

But somehow the invitation to dinner was different. It seemed so much more formal, especially when Mike casually threw in that the president of the college and his wife were also invited. She felt awkward about it somehow.

Mike said it was her fertile writer's imagination, drawing drama out of simple things, but no matter what he said, things *were* different now than the last time they had been together at the Tollivers, at least between her and Mike. The day of the ball game had been fun and friendship. *This is . . . this is what?* Mary frowned at her reflection in the mirror and pulled a different dress from her closet.

Her resolution to avoid analyzing the situation with Mike was weakening every day. She didn't want to subject it to scrutiny; she wanted to do exactly what she had said to Mike, to enjoy the loveliness of these weeks together. She didn't want the future to impose itself, to weigh down heavily on this lovely bubble in which she was living.

But the effort was wearing her out.

She heard the click of the front door and then a deep voice rolling down the hallway. "Mary?" Mike said. "Your doorbell's broken. You need a good handyman—" He was at the bedroom door now, his hands resting on the sides of the frame, his lean, long body filling it. She watched him at first in the mirror, took in the tailored slacks, the deep green V-neck sweater over his white turtleneck, the handsome sports jacket. His hair saved the image from being a page out of *GQ*. A few thick locks wandered lazily across his forehead, ready to be pushed back roughly when Mike absently forked his fingers through it.

"Go just like that," Mike said to her, his voice strangely thick. "You look perfect."

Mary turned around slowly.

The full white sweep of her throat was exquisite. Mike swallowed hard. He wanted to touch it, trace the graceful column with his fingers, down to the perfect cleavage visible through the delicate lace of her slip. Beneath his gaze she smiled unabashedly. That had been another surprise to him, her comfortableness with her body, although she admitted it had amazed *her,* as well, and that it must be the way Michael made her feel that allowed her such a luxury. "You don't judge me, Michael, that's what it is, I think." Mike had tucked that thought away, and wondered with some anger who had judged Mary with a harshness that caused her to fear it.

"You'd better get dressed, Mary," he said aloud.

"Are we late?"

"No, but we will be soon, if I look at you much longer like that."

She slipped on a softly gathered skirt and an ice blue silk blouse, ran a brush quickly through her hair, and announced herself ready. "I'm nervous, Michael, so know that ahead of time."

"So I can ward off any nervous comments? Mary, my love, why are you nervous? It's Polly and Stu—"

"*And* the president of the college and his wife."

"Not a big deal. They're old-shoe kind of folks, honest."

"I guess it's the two of us, going together—"

"I could follow you, if that'd help. Maybe come in an hour or two later. Say I had car trouble."

Mary stopped and let his teasing wash over her for a minute. Then she took a jacket from the closet and started for the door. "I don't know what it is, Mike. Maybe it's just that I'm not used to this."

"To what?"

"To having a . . . a relationship. In public."

Mike slipped her jacket over her shoulders and kissed her gently. "Is this my big-city girl I hear talking?" At that moment she was more important to him than he could remember anything being, ever.

"No, not at all," her voice was barely a whisper. "I don't know who this is, sometimes. I don't know who this is at all."

THE TOLLIVERS' big white house was lit up grandly when Mary and Mike arrived.

"At last!" Polly said, hugging Mary warmly. "Here I had to go and plan a fancy dig just to get to see you again!" Then she turned her small, charming face to Mike and scolded sternly. "You're hiding Mary from us again, Michael, and it simply won't work anymore. She likes us, Mike—"

Mary's nervousness evaporated beneath the lovely warmth of Polly's smile. Stu appeared then with a welcoming drink in his hand. He greeted Mary as if they had been friends for a lifetime, and then he took their coats and ushered them into the living room to join the other guests. Dancing flames reflected off the walls from the fire at the far end of the room. Seated in front of it were Bill Carroll and his wife, and in the worn leather chair skirting the fire was a man Mary did not recognize, and another woman sat across from him.

"John!" Mike said, striding across the patterned rug. "I didn't know you were going to be here."

The tall, angular man stood up and pumped Mike's hand. "Good to see you, Mike."

Polly brought in a plate of stuffed mushrooms and set them down on the coffee table. "Mary, come here and meet the Seavers. You're the reason they're here after all."

"Oh?" said Mike.

John Seaver laughed. He was in his late forties, a distinguished-looking gentleman with tiny laugh lines fanning out from his eyes and a sparkling of gray across a thick sweep of dark hair. He shook Mary's hand warmly and Stu finished the introductions. John and his wife, Nancy, were from Indianapolis and were in town for a meeting, Stu explained.

"I must confess, Mary," John said, "I *did* finagle the invitation."

"John is a closet novelist, Mary," said Nancy. She was a small blond woman, half her husband's size, with friendly blue eyes and a lovely laugh. "He's been dying to meet you."

"I think he thinks it will rub off on him, Mary," said Stu. "Kind of like fairy dust."

"Who knows?" John said with a laugh. "You take what you can get."

The whole group laughed then, and they made themselves comfortable, working quickly through the factual small talk of making new acquaintances, while Stu freshened drinks and Polly, gliding effortlessly between kitchen and living room, magically produced an elegant meal that soon lured them all into the dining room.

Mary looked around the old candlelit oak table and felt a sense of belonging that startled her. She barely knew these people, and yet, in an odd incredible way, she was a part of them.

Mike. It was Mike of course. They all adored Mike. And she was with Mike so they liked her, too. Oh, she knew it was not *just* that; they did want to know her, as well, to be her friend. But it all began with Mike.... *Her* Mike.

"So, Mary," Bill Carroll was saying, "you seem—how shall I say it?—*happy* here. Am I correct? Has the writing institute been a good experience for you?"

"It's been wonderful. And yes, Bill, I've been happy, indeed."

Mike's knee leaned into hers and the gentle pressure sent jolts of pleasure through her body.

And then Mike told them all about *Gideon's Gambit* and the award that Mary would be presented in just a few days.

"Mary, that's wonderful," Polly said. "How exciting and how proud you must be. When is the presentation?"

"I just heard today," she answered. "The dinner is the day after Thanksgiving."

"Not far off," said Sheila Carroll. "And such a festive time for it."

"Well, then," Polly said, picking up her wineglass, "I think this calls for a toast."

"A toast," repeated Stu. "Excellent idea, my dear." All glasses at the table were raised immediately in happy agreement.

"To Mary's award, to her success, and to her coming into our midst," Polly said, "and to her continual return—"

"I'll certainly drink to that," said Bill Carroll, and the sentiment was echoed around the table, from Sheila to Nancy Seaver to Stu and John. It passed like a gentle, rippling wave from one person to another as they sipped their wine and smiled at Mary, at one another.

Mary held her glass in the air and beside her Mike sat still, his fingers around his glass, his voice silent.

Mary felt suspended, waiting for something, for Mike to touch her, to say something, but there was only silence. She turned slightly, and saw then that he was watching her, his gaze washing over her, his eyes looking clear down into her soul. His face was calm, controlled, but his eyes were deep with a troubling emotion. A dull, nameless fear snaked through Mary and squeezed her heart, until she had to take a quick breath to release the pain. And then the voices around her grew louder, the laughter real again, and they moved on to manageable things, to toasting Polly's crown roast, then Bill's golf game and Stu's fixing of the twins' bikes, a mechanical first for the man of ten thumbs, as Polly called him. The gentle teasing washed over the group, and finally pushed away the moment that had frozen Mary's heart.

Over a velvety chocolate mousse dessert, Mary asked John about his writing.

"As Nancy so aptly put it, I'm a closet writer. It's what I want to do when I grow up—that sort of thing."

"There's no time like the present," Mary said encouragingly.

"Well, who knows, maybe one of these days. In the meantime I can dream."

"And write. It helps if you write while you dream," Mary said, and they all laughed.

Nancy patted John's hand. "Well, no matter who publishes them, *I* think his stories are wonderful. And until we get the kids through college it might be just as well that he stick to his profession.''

"And what is that?" Mary asked politely.

"Ophthalmology," John said, and Sheila Carroll added, "John is at the University Med Center in Indianapolis. One of the finest doctors we have there."

Mary looked over at Mike, but he was busy arguing with Polly about an old rock group they used to follow in college. She turned back to John. "You might know Mike's brother Andy, then—"

"I sure do. I know Andy well. He's crazy, as those Gibsons are, but one of my brightest interns this year. Which reminds me—" He looked over at Mike, then paused, seemed to change his mind, and said to Mary, "Anyway, he's a great fellow and he'll make a fine doctor. I think there's something in the Gibson genes—in spite of their wild oats, they all end up being great guys."

Mike tuned in at the end of the sentence and laughed. "Hey, John, I could tell a tale or two about you—"

Stu pitched in then and the three of them entertained with wild tales of days spent at the college together, when Mike and Stu, still in high school, used to work in one of the offices and learned the facts of life by following the love lives of John and his frat brothers.

Nancy shook her head and rolled her eyes. "Will they ever change, Polly?"

"No, and we wouldn't have it any other way." She made an affectionate face at Stu.

"You know, speaking of Andy Gibson," John said then, "he's actually the one who told me about you, Mary."

"Me? But—"

Mike laughed. "Sorry, Mary, but in the Gibson clan, nothing is sacred, not what you eat, who you see, what you do—"

"Andy said great things about you," John said.

"But we've never met!"

"See what I mean?" said Mike, and they all laughed.

"The family sends reports," John went on. "They have this incredible system—"

"Okay, enough," laughed Mike. "You'll scare her."

"Listen," Mary said, "I've known you long enough now that nothing would surprise me." The gentle teasing went back and forth until Polly rose to clear the dishes, shooing everyone away from the table. "There's a pot of coffee in the living room for seconds," she said, "and a bottle of brandy for anyone who would like some."

There was a flurry of activity, people clearing the table, getting themselves glasses of water in the kitchen, rinsing dishes. Mike slipped an arm around Mary and squeezed her gently into his side as she walked through the door. "You okay?"

She nodded.

"Good. Just don't believe everything they say," he said with a slow smile.

John Seaver walked into the kitchen balancing a stack of dessert dishes on his arm. "Hey, Mike, I nearly forgot, did you get the glasses?"

Mike nodded and took some of the dishes from him while Mary began helping Polly stack.

"Are they helping?" he asked in a low voice.

"Fine," Mike said.

"I brought some drops that will help at night."

"Thanks."

Mary heard the words dimly, not really putting them together until after John and Mike walked out of the room together. She glanced over at Polly. "Polly, what did John mean?"

"What?" Polly looked up from the sink.

"John was talking to Mike about drops and sunglasses, in kind of a serious way."

"John is entertaining and funny, but when he's talking medicine, he's all business."

"But they were just sunglasses that Mike's brother sent. Some freebies, I guess, that he passed along to Mike. What do you mean, business?"

Polly looked at Mary for a minute, then said slowly, "Well, John is Mike's doctor, so it was probably a little more than just sunglasses," and then she moved swiftly and purposefully across the room and pulled out a tray. "Will you help me with this, Mary?" she said, and began piling it with bowls of mints and small chocolates.

And before Mary could pursue the subject, Polly had urged her back into the living room and the sea of animated, laughing voices, but not before Mary saw the frustrated look clouding her hostess's lively green eyes.

It was much later when John and Nancy reluctantly stood and announced they had to be on their way.

"We've an hour's ride ahead of us, and my singing will keep John awake for just so long," Nancy said.

The Seavers departed with promises to be in touch, and the rest of the group began to make moves to leave, weary yet unwilling to let go of the evening's pleasure. Mike helped Polly take the trays into the kitchen while Mary went to retrieve their coats.

When she headed toward the kitchen to get Mike, the door was partially closed and she heard Polly's voice, serious now, without the merriment of the evening coloring it.

"You're not playing fair, Mike," she was saying. Her voice was low and clear.

Mary frowned, unsure of whether or not to go in. Polly sounded irritated and she didn't want to step into the middle of a personal argument between her and Mike.

"Mary doesn't know, does she?" Polly went on, and Mary felt her heart skip a beat. She took a step away. She felt like an eavesdropper, and a faint blush touched her cheeks.

"Polly, listen," Mike said, "there's absolutely no reason to saddle Mary with my problems—"

"No reason? She's *in love with you,* damn it! Can't you see that, you big galoot!"

Just then Bill Carroll came into the hallway. "Mary!" he said. "Just the person I'm looking for—" And he proceeded to tell her how happy Dr. Atwood was with her workshop, and that they were receiving enthusiastic comments from the students as well. "The students think you're a breath of fresh air," he said, "and I've no doubt at all that they are absolutely right."

Mary thanked him graciously, barely hearing his words, her mouth working independently of her heart. The fear was back, an irrational vice, squeezing the air out of her lungs.

"Are you all right, Mary? You look a little pale?" he asked solicitously.

Mary forced a smile. "I'm fine, Bill, thank you. Just tired, is all."

The door opened and Mike came into the hallway. "Ready to go?" he asked. He was somber, his eyes without the laughter Mary always looked for in the familiar blue sea. For all the hours she had spent with Mike in the past few weeks, she had rarely seen worry in his eyes; tonight it was there, as stark and clear as the night sky.

CONVERSATION ON THE WAY back to Mary's was subdued and unmemorable. Mary was lost in thought. She had no idea what Polly and Mike had been talking about, but the words were rolling around in her head, one phrase and then another. They each demanded her attention, but the words that rose to the top and grew to enormous dimensions were those simple, unexpressed, unaudited, unalterable ones: *She loves you...*

And she did. Absolutely and completely. Thinking back now she was not sure when it happened. It could have happened that night in the Laundromat, a lifetime ago, or it could have been yesterday. But it did not matter; what mattered was that it was absolutely true, without a doubt. Hearing it said, flung out into the reality of the world like that, had given it an existence apart from her mind and her heart. It was a *real* thing, an entity. And that fact frightened and excited her.

She looked over at Mike, at the pensive expression on his face. He was deep in his own thoughts, whatever they were. Yes, she loved him. She *loved* him. Wholly and wonderfully, and she knew with a certainty that startled her, that nothing—*nothing*—could change that fact.

Mike pulled the car up to the curb in front of Mary's house. "Mary—" he started.

Mary looked over at him.

"Oh, Mary—" His heart was so full, so painfully full. For a long time now he had worked on making his life as uncomplicated as possible. *Obstacle free.* Those were his operating words. And now, now there was Mary.

Mary looked at him for a long time, and then she smiled, and he saw in her smile the acknowledgment of everything Polly had said. He saw there the breadth and depth, the intensity of all their feelings for one another encapsulated in a single, loving look. Without a word, Mary slipped out of the car and, in unspoken agreement, Mike followed her inside. Whatever the complications were, they would have to be put aside for this night. This night they needed each other.

They left the house dark, bathed only in moonlight, and walked silently back to the small bedroom, to the wide, quilt-covered bed.

With a slant of yellow moonlight to guide their way, they slipped out of their clothes and left them in a heap on the floor, then crawled into bed together.

For a long time Mike simply held her, his arms wrapped around her in great tenderness, her head resting against his chest. He dropped kisses on the top of her head, and in the sensitive hollow of her neck. And when the need became bigger than either one of them, they moved together swiftly.

Mike reached out for her, clung to her as they climbed each new height together. But this night their lovemaking was different somehow, filled with a raw, almost desperate, need that made Mary tremble.

And for long hours afterward, he lay awake beside Mary's lovely sleeping form, wading through the labyrinth of his emotions. He stared up at the ceiling as if he'd find some answers there. But he wouldn't, of course.

If there were any, it was going to have to be in a far more profound place.

Chapter Eleven

For the next few days, Mike worked on his thoughts like an artist with a thick hunk of clay, trying to mold it into something satisfying. But the only thing that made sense was Mary. Being with her. Loving her. After agonizing hours, hours spent walking alone in the woods behind his house, he realized the truth of it all—he did love her. What had begun so innocently—a simple friendship, that's what they had pledged to one another—had somehow deepened into this.

And for the first time in his life, Mike didn't know what to do.

Mary made no demands, spoke little about the future, seemed satisfied with each day and the joy that it brought to both of them. Watching her, loving her, he convinced himself that certainly everyone in his lifetime is owed that one joyous time when neither plans nor future matter, when the present can be enjoyed to its fullest without thought of what lies ahead.

"MIKE," MARY SAID one day, "I've been thinking about something."

Mike looked up. He was sitting on a log near the stream that ran through the center of campus, reading a book. It was cold, the end of autumn, and they had bundled up and brought blankets so they could enjoy the last of the magnificent color that painted the campus with a palette of crimson and gold and brilliant oranges.

Mary sat beside him, a heavy parka pulled up to her chin and her back resting against a gnarled oak tree. She was trying to write comments on her students' short stories, but her mind was wandering. "I was thinking about my trip to New York."

Mike had thought about it, too, ever since she had mentioned it at the Tollivers'. It was next week, and then she came back for two weeks, and then the semester was over. The workshop was over. And the fantasy life they'd forged out of the Indiana countryside was over.

"Would you come with me?" she asked.

"Come with you?"

"Yes," she nodded, holding back her excitement. She'd presented this casually, but she had given it a lot of thought, outlining in her mind the wonderful reasons for his going. First of all, four days away from Mike would be agony. She couldn't imagine it, couldn't fathom what the world would look like to her without Mike being there. And he was the one person in the world with whom she cared about sharing this award.

She wanted Mike to be proud with her, *for* her. But beneath it all was the insane hope that seeing her in *her* world, sharing in it with her for however brief a time, would finally open them up to discuss the future.

There *was* a future together, of that Mary was certain now. She refused to allow herself to think otherwise. She loved Mike, and he loved her, she was as certain of that as of her own existence. It was in his eyes, in his voice and it was confirmed forever in the incredible tenderness with which he loved her. They hadn't talked about plans or commitments, but they would have to soon. She looked back at Mike. "I'm flying out after my class on Wednesday. I would love for you to come along, to be there at the dinner Friday night, to be at my side. I...it would make it complete, Mike."

"But, Mary, I—"

"And we'd have the whole weekend together, Mike," she rushed on, not allowing his objection to formulate itself. "We'd have all the time in the world to play in New York, to have fun. We'd stay at my apartment, of course, and go out to dinner, to a play or two. We'd have a glorious time, Mike. We would—"

"Mary, I'd love to see the presentation, you know that. I'd be the proudest person there, but—"

"Wait, Mike, don't say yes or no. Just tell me you'll think about it. We'd have a wonderful time, I know we would. We could be together for four marvelous days, without the disruptions of classes and work. We could get up at two in the afternoon, or stay in bed all day if we wanted to, or dance all night or—"

Mike was laughing now. "My hopeless romantic."

"Of course I am! And I owe it all to you. I was never this way, Mike Gibson, nope." She got up and walked around behind him, bending down and wrapping her arms around him. "No, I was never this way until I fell under your crazy Hoosier spell."

Her breath was hot on the skin of his neck and the clean, soapy smell of her hair wafted about him. She was making it very difficult to think. "You're a vixen, Mary. A wicked woman, a—"

Her laughter, a lilting sound caught up on the breeze, swept away his words. "That's the nicest thing you could say to me, Michael." She kissed the top of his head. "The very nicest thing. Now, do I have your word?"

"Yes, I'll think about it."

"You'll think positively about it?"

He slipped off his sunglasses, looked at her solemnly and nodded. "You're persistent, I'll say that much."

"And don't you ever forget it." She lifted her head back then and gazed at him gravely for a minute. Then her lips turned up slightly at the corners.

Mike leaned down. "A vixen, a hussy, a..." He breathed, and then there were no words left, only the gentle press of her slightly parted lips.

IT WAS NOT UNTIL the weekend that Mike told Mary he couldn't go with her to New York. The decision hadn't come easily.

Friday he had driven alone to Indianapolis. The morning was spent going through the usual battery of tests on his eyes with John Seaver.

"There doesn't seem to be much change, Mike," John had said, "but of course we'll know for sure when the tests are in. But for now things look okay—"

"Things look okay?" Mike had said, then followed it up with a short, hollow laugh.

"I'm sorry, Mike, there isn't more I can say."

"I know, John, I know. It's just that my life has taken some turns lately, unexpected ones, and it's thrown my jolly control all to hell."

"Mary?"

He nodded.

"Enough to throw any man's jolly control to hell. Lovely lady, Mike. You're lucky."

"Lucky to have had this time with her, yes. But she leads a different life, John. She's not cut out for what I could offer her."

"Are you sure?"

"About as sure as I've ever been of anything."

"You know Mary far better than I do, Mike. But be careful," he had said. "Don't ever sell anyone short. Worst thing you can do to a person—"

Mike nodded. Essentially, he believed what John was saying. But what John didn't know was the kind of life Mary had had, sequestered in a godforsaken town just as she was waking up as a woman, wanting to taste everything, to savor all that life had to offer. No, it was to Mike, her friend, that Mary had poured out her heart and her dreams. It was to Mike that she had confided in the kind of life she wanted, the kind she had to have to make up for those years of her life. Only Mike knew that. And that was the sad, awful truth.

Andy met him for lunch in the hospital cafeteria.

"Hey, my man, when do I get to meet her?" Andy's tawny hair fell across his forehead as he talked. Mike liked being with his youngest brother. He was so upfront, honest, and he still believed that he could do anything, have anything, be anything his heart desired. Fortunately, his dad often said, that desirable something right now was being a doctor, rather than the world's greatest stunt artist. It had been a toss-up for a while.

"You can meet her anytime. Come around," Mike said with a quiet smile. "Mary'd like to meet you, too. But you'd better do it soon. She leaves at the end of the semester."

"Leaves?"

"Goes back to New York, or wherever. Mary has lots of plans."

"I don't understand. I thought—I mean, the folks are under the impression you care a whole lot about this woman."

"I do."

"Then why—"

"Different lives. It wouldn't work. We have a great thing right now, *terrific*, as a matter of fact. She's... well, she's lovely, Andy. She's incredible. And she makes *me* feel incredible. But some things, even incredulous, once-in-a-lifetime happenings like this, aren't forever kinds of things. Sometimes it just works out that way."

"So you say thanks for the memories and goodbye?"

Mike winced. It sounded cold and harsh coming out of Andy's mouth that way. And it wasn't the truth, not entirely. It wasn't just the memories that would stay behind. It was the love. He'd always love her, that was one of the few things these days he was sure of.

Talking it over with Andy and John, even on a superficial level, helped him. Saying the truth out loud, as matter-of-factly as one talked about jobs and business deals, put it in its place, removed, at least for the moment, the gut-wrenching emotion that grounded it all.

Going to New York with Mary would not be fair to her, he reasoned on the drive back to Chestershire. It would strengthen the ties, becoming a part of that other world that was hers, complicating the already intricate web they'd spun around themselves. He was an Indiana handyman to Mary, and it would be far easier for her to say goodbye to *that* Mike than to one who had been a part of her New York life, even if only for a weekend.

But when he told Mary, the disappointment in her eyes caused his resolve to falter.

"Mike, it would mean so much to me," she said. They were at Mike's house, ensconced in front of the fire Mike had built to ward off an onslaught of unexpected northerly winds.

"An early winter," Mike had told her, "at least that's what the *Farmers' Almanac* claims. But," he had added as he lit the fire, "winter's more fun, anyway. Such a good excuse to find innovative ways to keep warm—"

Now Mike's eyes were gazing into the leaping mass of flames. One arm rested on the back of the couch and his fingers played with her hair as he talked. "Mary, *I'm* the one disappointed. I would like to see you honored. That would mean a lot to me, but there are too many reasons why it would be better for me to stay here. Thanksgiving being one—"

"Thanksgiving..." Mary spoke the word with great attention. "I understand that your whole family gets together on Thanksgiving and that that's important to you. But maybe you could fly in after dinner that day, or even early on Friday. That would still give us the weekend—"

"There're things to do here, and family will be here the whole weekend. It's a bad time, that's all," he said.

Mary's shoulders dropped. She had had it all planned out in her head, all the things they would do, what they'd see. She was so eager to share it all with him.

Mike's hand dropped onto her shoulder. He hated to see her sad. He'd do anything to put a smile on her face. "I'm sorry, Mary. I think it's better this way. You need to go back and touch your roots again, polish up those goals of yours."

Her eyes reflected the firelight and the tiny specks of gold danced as he looked into them. She was listening so carefully to his words.

"Mike," she said finally, resting her hand on his thigh, "my goals *are* intact. As much as I've loved all this Hoosier hospitality, it hasn't changed that. I still want to succeed as a writer. I still *will* do that, and I will fill my life with an abundance of experiences." She was smiling. "Of course I will do that, and now there's you, too, an experience I never dreamed about."

"So that's what I am to you," he said, "an experience."

"The best of all of them—" She leaned her head onto his shoulder. There was such comfort now in his presence, such grounding. It was something Mary had never missed before because in all her life she had never had it. But she did now, she did with Mike. She turned her head slightly and kissed his shoulder.

"What's that for?" He smiled down at her.

"For nothing, for everything."

"Hm-m-m—"

"For all these weeks of a kind of peace and joy I've never known before."

"It's been like that for me, too, you know. This isn't a one-way track we've thrown ourselves on."

"I know." Her words were as soft as a butterfly's wing.

"In fact," Mike went on, "you've given me the best weeks of my life."

The words were said with such urgency that they startled Mary for a minute. Then she smoothed them over, forced a lightness into them and vehemently threw out the fear that briefly flickered in her heart. "And, buster," she said in her best gun-moll voice, "you ain't seen nothin' yet!"

And with an overwhelming passion that Michael could not have imagined coming from the delicate, slender woman with whom he was falling deeply in love, Mary began to show him.

MARY DID NOT BRING UP the trip again, even though Mike knew how keenly she wanted him to go with her. He vacillated between guilt and justice, firmly believing that in the end he was doing right by Mary by not going. It would give them some time apart, and when she came back she would feel differently; she would be grounded again in her world and what she wanted from it. She would see more clearly that for her these weeks with Mike were a kind of hiatus in her life, but that what she wanted was far different, far broader than anything she could ever get from a long-term commitment to Mike Gibson.

On Wednesday afternoon, Mike drove her up to Indianapolis to the airport. They stood together, clouded in an unusual silence, while an airline staff member announced the boarding of her plane.

"Well," Mary said, "I'll see you soon—" She pushed a smile onto her face, but her bottom lip quivered.

Mike was standing so close to her she could have whispered the words. "Hey, this is a happy day," he said. "Focus in on the literary award, the glory of it all."

"Glory isn't my game, Mike."

He held her shoulders and looked down at her. "No, no it's not. I'm sorry, Mary, I was trying to lighten the moment."

Mary brushed her hand across her eyes. "I'm tired, I guess. Tired and afraid, Mike."

"Of what?"

"I don't know. You, us, maybe. I'm frightened of the fact that we've never discussed beyond today, beyond this minute. It's like an unwritten pact between us, somehow, that we won't force what we have between us to stand up to the light of the real day, of reality, of todays that have tomorrows—" She shook her head then, frowned. "Damn! This was truly awful of me, to throw this all out in front of you when I have to turn around in five seconds and walk onto the plane."

"Yes," and that was all Mike had time to say before Mary spun around and hurried through the gate.

He turned slowly and walked out of the airport and to his car. And then, on sudden impulse, he drove into Indianapolis. Before returning to Chestershire, Mike ordered three dozen long-stemmed roses to be presented to Mary Shields at the writers' awards dinner at the Raphael Hotel, wired her a bottle of champagne, and then, as an afterthought, called F.A.O. Schwarz and had a giant plush-toy turkey sent to her apartment. At least with the turkey he'd be there in spirit.

SIX OUT OF THE SEVEN Gibson offspring were present at Thanksgiving dinner, a fact that brought unbounded joy to Marie and Stan. The grandchildren scampered about, the noise of parades blared from the television set, and the mingled scents of turkey, oyster stuffing, cranberries and pumpkin pie deliciously filled the whole house.

"It's too bad Mary couldn't have joined us," Marie said to Mike as he helped her lift the giant bird from the oven.

"Yeah," Mike said.

"I remember the year Dani came," Marie went on. "We overwhelmed her."

"A little. Dani was always more comfortable with a uniformed waiter at her side. She couldn't quite figure out the mechanics of clearing dishes and all that."

"Well, Mary would have been different."

Would she have been? Mike wondered. And then just as quickly the thought disappeared. Yes, Mary would have been different. Her first trip to the Gibson household had been awkward for her. But each subsequent time had been easier, more comfortable for Mary, and he knew she had come to look forward to seeing his family. It was a new world for her, to be sucked into a large family that wouldn't leave her alone, that insisted she be a part of it, that she hug and laugh and cry with them. It was a dimension to "family" she hadn't known growing up, and she was slowly but willingly becoming acclimated to it.

She had told him on the way to the airport that she and her father had never celebrated Thanksgiving. "I guess Thanksgiving isn't for two," she had said, "It's for a whole bunch of people, and we weren't ever a whole bunch of people."

Mike thought about that now, as he listened to the pleasant sounds bouncing off the walls in this house, of the squabbles and hugs and sporadic shrieks of laughter, as he watched his father sitting quietly in his big armchair watching all the chaos and loving every minute of it.

And he thought of Mary in New York.

"Is she alone there? Will she be with friends today?" Marie asked him now.

"In New York? I don't know, Mom, I don't know."

"Well, you could go in right now and call her. Then you would know."

Mike laughed at his mother's directness. He hugged her lightly and escaped to a phone that was tucked beneath the stairs in a spot that was relatively quiet. When Mary didn't answer, he was relieved, and then he was saddened. Hearing her voice would have helped fill the empty spot inside him, which no amount of turkey and stuffing and homemade pie could even begin to touch.

They finished dinner by two, a family tradition that left time for the raucous touch football game, brisk walks for some and naps for others, before they brought out the home movies and leftovers later that night.

Mike was leaning against the wall in the back hall, watching the kids rummage through the pile of sweat-shirts, hats and gloves for the game, when his father tapped him on his shoulder and nodded toward the den. "Join me?"

Mike followed him into the cozy room that always smelled faintly of pipe tobacco and settled himself in the warm leather chair near his father's desk. "What's up, Pop?"

"Just wanted a moment alone with you, to kind of touch base, see how things are going."

"Fine, Dad. Everything's okay. Andy's filled you in on the medical side of my life, I'm sure—"

Stan nodded. "He stays right on top of all those damn tests they put you through. And we're lucky he does. He's a good fellow, Andy is."

"And John Seaver is a good doctor. They're doing what they can, Pop."

"I know that." His dad leaned back in the chair and sighed. Mike watched him and wished his father did not have to go through all this. Sometimes he thought the damn disease was harder on him than on Mike himself. It seemed to age him, take the wind out of his sails.

"And now there's Mary in your life," Stan Gibson said slowly.

Mike was silent.

"Your mother says she wanted you to go to New York with her, some award she's getting."

Mike nodded.

"Why didn't you?"

"There've been a lot of moments since yesterday afternoon when I'll be damned if I know, Pop. It seemed the best decision at the time."

"Life's short, son."

"And full of complications. Nothing's simple, is it?"

"Nope, but there are some simple rules. Be there, when people need you. Share joys and sorrows, all that sort of thing. And don't avoid problems, meet them head on. You've always done that, Mike—"

Mike leaned forward, his elbows on his knees. He looked down at his hands. There were some calluses on his palms from chopping a huge pile of firewood late yesterday. The chore had been a release, a catharsis of sorts, and he rubbed the hardened knobs absently now. Finally he looked up and said, "There's a plane around five."

Stan nodded. "That's true. And I think the troops will do nicely without their halfback. Give Andy a chance to be the hero."

Mike nodded. His dad stood and walked over to Mike. He rested his hand on his eldest son's shoulder for just a minute, then gave it a quick squeeze and walked out of the room.

His mother was alone in the kitchen when he walked in.

She smiled at him the way she used to do when he went a week without getting called into the principal's office. "You know what I say, Mike?" she asked.

"What Mom?"

"*You*, Michael, take care of today. Take care of it and make the most of it. And you leave the future to more competent sources." She lifted her eyes heavenward.

"Yeah, Mom." He hugged her gently. "I know that's what you say."

BY THE TIME THE 747 touched down at JFK, Mike had his plans formulated. It helped pass the time, calm the jumble of emotions cartwheeling around inside him. Tonight he'd surprise her; tomorrow they'd attend the dinner together, and Saturday they would talk. That was where he had failed in all this, the talking, and now the time had definitely come.

The streets were surprisingly hushed for New York. Department stores and apartment houses were lit up like Christmas trees and the streets were lined with cars as the cab sped through a tranquil black Thanksgiving night. Mike smiled in anticipation as the cab driver slowed down and hunted for Mary's address. He peered through the smudged window, searching himself, but the addresses were too dim to make out. Damn, another limitation creeping in. Bright sunlight drove him to sunglasses and now the soothing darkness of night made it almost impossible to see details. Everything blurred. He frowned, sat back and let the cab driver grapple with the addresses.

The apartment building was red brick and squeezed in between a dozen others that varied only in the color of the awnings or the number of air-conditioning units that stuck out of the windows.

Mike stood out in front and looked up. Mary. She was up there somewhere, behind one of those curtained windows. His heart quickened and he bounded up the concrete steps two at a time. In a small glassed-in foyer were two rows of small square speakers. Mary's name was in the second row, M. Shields, printed neatly below a speaker. Second floor, 202, it said. Mike pressed the buzzer and waited.

After three or more tries he decided she might be in the shower. It was nearly ten now, she was probably getting ready for bed. He'd give her ten minutes, then try again.

TWENTY MINUTES LATER Mike leaned up against the wall and wondered what to do. He could flag a cab, get a hotel room and call Mary. Or—

Just then an elderly woman peered out of a door on the first level, staring at Mike through the glass doors. She adjusted her glasses, then looked at him again. Finally she shoved open the heavy glass foyer door and asked if she could help him.

"I'm here to see Mary Shields. I came from Indiana—"

The woman smiled. "Indiana, yes, Mary is teaching there."

Mike was encouraged. He went on. "She doesn't answer her buzzer. Would you know if she's in?"

"I know she won't answer her buzzer, that much I know," the gray-haired lady said, shaking her head. "The buzzers are all broken. Happened this morning when Jake—he does odd jobs around here for me—when he was trying to fix the washing machines. Jake isn't too handy but he's cheap. They'll be fixed soon enough, but with Thanksgiving and all we couldn't get it done today."

"I see. Is there any chance I could come in and knock on her door?"

"No, you can't do that. You look nice enough, but I can't let you do that, no. Besides, Mary's not up there."

Mike frowned.

"She went out for a bite to eat with her agent. Mary's a writer, don't you know? We chatted a bit before she left. She brought me some apple butter from Indiana, you see. Now she'll be back before too long—" The woman checked a large-faced watch on her wrist and squinted at the numbers. "She'll be back here in an hour or so, young man. You come back then. That's her apartment right above you. Front left." Before Michael could comment, the woman had disappeared behind her apartment door and the thick glass door separating him from the warm hallway had clicked closed and locked.

Mike checked his watch and rubbed the side of his head. He was dead tired, but he wanted to see her tonight, to be with her. He'd come this far—the hell with cabs and hotels. He had seen a diner around the corner; he would go over, load up on coffee, then be waiting on the steps when she returned. And then they'd have a homecoming for just the two of them. A genuine Thanksgiving homecoming.

The waitress glared at him when he walked in. Mike smiled brightly. Poor kid, working in a dump like this on Thanksgiving night. He would have to remember to leave her a few bills. She brought him coffee and managed a small smile when he convinced her leaving the pot with him would save her steps and make them both happier, and then Mike settled back in the cold plastic booth in the diner and closed his eyes.

He thought of that very first time, that night in the Laundromat . . . that night a full lifetime ago when life was so simple. His lips curved into a half smile as the memories flooded back and the warmth and joy of the whole incredible thing seeped slowly into his bones.

"Hey, mister, you okay?"

Mike felt a rough jostling of his arm. His eyes shot open. He jolted upright.

"Hey, sorry, but you looked out cold," the young girl said. "I thought maybe you passed out or something. Except," she frowned at him, "except for that smile you had. Guys who pass out in here don't smile."

Michael focused in on her and his surroundings began to register. The diner, of course. "I guess I fell asleep," he said.

"I guess. A long time ago, too. Coffee's all cold and we're lockin' up."

"A long time…Damn!" Mike glanced at the round clock high on the wall and slid quickly out of the booth.

The waitress jumped back. "Hey, it's okay."

"No, it's not. I'm late. Here—" He slapped a ten-dollar bill in her hand, grabbed his overnight bag and rushed out of the diner.

In two minutes he was around the corner, across the street, and standing on the deserted sidewalk in front of Mary's apartment building. The second-floor apartment on the left was bathed in a soft golden light.

Damn, he'd missed her! She was already home, already up there in her apartment, safe behind locked doors and mute intercom speakers. He shoved his hands into his pockets and stared at the windows. A cold wind whipped some crumpled paper down the street and it slapped against his pant leg but he did not notice. She was so close, right there, behind those blinds.

The ground-floor apartments were all dark, including that of the older woman with whom he had talked before. Asleep, he thought. It was nearly midnight;

they were probably all asleep. All except Mary, right up there just a stone's throw away.

A stone's throw! Yes, that just might do it. As a kid he had had quite a reputation for slingshot expertise. This would be a breeze. His heart lifted.

Mike checked out the three or four windows that seemed to be Mary's apartment, then decided to try the one in the small alley on the side. The light was brighter there, and it was more protected; he would be less likely to attract attention. He bent over and scooped up a handful of gravel, then took aim. The first stone hit the protruding windowsill and Michael stepped back a little farther. The windows were higher than he had thought. The next stone was larger, smoother, and his aim was perfect. With a resounding ping it hit the window, then bounced off. Mike waited, his eyes glued to the window. For a minute he thought he saw a shadow, then nothing.

He shot again. Three or four of his stones went askew, hitting the brick wall of the building, but most were right on target, plinking off Mary's window rhythmically. Mike shivered; he wrapped his arms around himself, rubbed briskly and waited. It was freezing, colder than in Indiana, and the black night carried eerie noises and the smell of grease from a restaurant down the street.

He picked up another stone, stood as poised as a javelin thrower, then stretched his arm back to throw.

"Freeze! Hold it right there, buddy!"

Mike's heart stopped. The stone clattered to the ground.

"Keep your arms in the air and turn around, *v-e-r-y* slowly!" a new voice, this one a thick authoritative voice, commanded.

"Oh, hell," Mike murmured. Then slowly he rotated his freezing body toward the voices. A blinding light was shining directly at him and instinctively he covered his eyes.

"Arms up!" the voice demanded.

Mike closed his eyes and lifted his arms slowly. "Hey, who are you guys?" he asked, forcing a calmness into his voice.

"Police. The interesting question is who are you?"

"Mike. Mike Gibson. I'm visiting here—" He tried to get his wallet out but the policeman moved closer, the light still aimed at his eyes. He couldn't see anything at all.

"Sorry, buddy—" the bodiless voice said, "—but your fun and games are over."

Before Mike could see the man's face he was behind him, pulling his arms down and slapping the cold steel bracelets around his wrists.

"Hey, this is crazy! It's a mistake! Just let me explain."

"Oh, you'll have plenty of time to explain, in considerable detail. Plenty of time. Shame on you, disturbing people on Thanksgiving. Don't you have any decency, you peeping toms, you— What the hell is the world coming to anyway!"

Mike tried to explain again in the car, but no one seemed to care that he was from Indiana, just flew in unexpectedly, and he knew the lady who lived in the second-story apartment. Even when they booked him, no one seemed particularly interested; in fact, he vaguely suspected no one had ever *heard* of Indiana, especially when the jailer told him he was surprised he didn't have darker skin and black hair.

It was a while later before Mike got to the phone. His fingers were smudged with ink, his head ached and he was beginning to wonder about the wisdom of his mother's advice. The day might have been a hell of a lot nicer if he had left it alone.

He dialed Mary's number.

THE PHONE WAS RINGING, when Mary stepped out of the shower. Her heart lurched. Mike! Maybe he had called after all. She had almost refused her agent's suggestion that they go out for a sandwich because she thought he might call while she was gone. But practicality won out: she was starving, there was nothing to eat in her refrigerator, and she missed Michael so much she thought she was beside herself. So she'd gone, rushed back, and then finally called his house and sat in silence with her enormous toy turkey on her lap while the phone rang and rang and rang.

"Hello?" she said now.

"Happy Thanksgiving, darlin'."

"Michael! Oh, Mike—" Her hand went to her throat and then she laughed at her breathlessness. "It's so wonderful to hear your voice, Mike."

"Is it wonderful enough for me to ask a small favor of you, Mare?"

"Of course. Anything, Mike."

"Any chance you'd like to take a ride down to the Forty-third Precinct? I'm in jail."

Chapter Twelve

Mary sat on a bench in the drafty gray room, waiting for him. The desk sergeant had given her a cup of coffee and she cradled the mug in her hands now, letting its warmth seep into her shaking fingers.

A small noise drew her attention to the door at the far side of the room. Mike stood there—his hair was mussed, his eyes bleary, his hands shoved in his pockets. He grinned at her crookedly. "Hey, kiddo, what's a nice girl like you doing in a place like this?"

"It's the company I keep," she said. A lump was forming in her throat. In the single day she had been away from him, his presence had taken on enormous proportions in her mind. Seeing him now, so unexpectedly, was almost more than she could bear. Could she attack him here in the middle of the police station? Her palms began to itch, her insides tighten. *Oh, Michael Gibson,* she cried silently, *what have you done to me?*

"How about a turkey leg?" the desk sergeant said. He leaned across the desk, his thick forearms pressing into the worn, scratched wood and he smiled congenially at both of them.

Mary shook her head, her eyes still on Mike. Mike looked at the sergeant, at Mary, back to the sergeant. He smiled crookedly and said, "Hey, maybe I will. I've worked up quite an appetite tonight."

"Eat?" Mary squeaked.

Mike shrugged, then looked at the policeman with a feigned look of great regret. "Guess not, sarge. Thanks anyway." He nodded toward Mary and said in a conspiratory whisper, "You know women."

The sergeant winked knowingly. "Yeah, sure. I understand. And I hope you understand about tonight. Sorry about the little mess-up. Those guys were rookies, good officers, but real zealous types. You know what I mean?"

"No problem," Mike said. "Mary and I'll sleep better knowing they're out there."

Mary was off the bench and had his arm now. "Any chance you two could continue this conversation another time?"

"Well, now, little lady, we figure we owe this fellow a few amenities, seeing as how we brought him down here on Thanksgiving, and all."

"And he thanks you graciously for them." She looked at Mike. "Don't you, Michael—"

"Graciously," Mike said, his eyes on Mary's face. His voice was husky, deep in his throat.

"Good, then we can leave. Good night, officer." She nudged Michael toward the door.

Michael looked back over his shoulder. "Thanks, sarge. It was nice meeting you."

"My pleasure," said the amiable policeman. "And a happy Thanksgiving to you both. And little lady, I'd say you owe him a few amenities yourself, keeping him locked out in the cold like that and all." He winked again.

"I'll see to it," Mary shot back without turning around. "You have my solemn word!" And she let the door bang shut behind her.

IT WAS NEARLY one-thirty in the morning when Mary and Mike stumbled through the doors of Mary's apartment, their arms tight around each other.

"I can't believe you're here," Mary murmured, her head inches from his chest.

"Easily proved," he said, tipping her head back and drawing her close to kiss her.

Finally they pulled apart and Mary looked up at him. "But *why*, Mike? Why are you here?" Her eyes were moist.

Mike took off her coat, then his own and dropped them on a chair. He drew her to him on the small love seat near the window. "Reasons probably don't matter a lot, Mary. I needed to be here, that's all. We needed some time together away from Chestershire. Time to talk. Mostly I wanted to be here tomorrow night for you, to see you receive the award."

"Today," Mary corrected. "Tomorrow is today." She snuggled into his side. "I missed you, Mike. Even

with Hoosier here to keep me company, I missed you.''
Mike looked across the room. Seated on a rug in front
of the fireplace, its two legs stuck straight out in front
of him, was a huge plush turkey.

"Hoosier," Mike repeated, then laughed.

"He's great," she said. "Wonderful company—"

"Looks like he has center stage. Do I have competition?"

"What do you think?" she said, and she slipped her
hands beneath his shirt, running them over his warm
skin, playing with the springy tangle of hair on his
chest.

Mike's breathing quickened. He closed his eyes and
held her close. "Thinking isn't one of my strong points
tonight, darlin'. Does it matter...?"

Mary shook her head slowly against his shoulder.
No, no, it did not matter at all. Nothing mattered right
now except the fact that Mike was here at her side, his
warmth seeping into her, blocking out the coldness of
the crisp November night, the chill of the fear she had
been left with at the airport all those hours ago.

She slipped from his embrace, stood and took his
hand. And then she led him quietly into the next room.

WHEN MIKE AWOKE hours later, Mary was silhouetted
at the window in the small high-ceilinged bedroom, the
morning sunshine bright behind her. She held a cup of
coffee as she gazed out at the street below. He watched
her in silence.

Finally she turned, her eyes seeking his. "I felt you," she said.

Mike nodded. The unspoken links between them had been real for a while now: the phone that rang as he thought of her, the sentences they finished for each other, the way Mary often mentioned a story or a piece of music just as he was thinking about it.

"Hungry?" she asked.

"A leading question..."

"I know. I want you again. Isn't that ridiculous?"

"No."

"But the day is slipping away from us. There are so many things I want to show you."

"You don't have to, Mary. I'm here for you, not to use you as a tour guide."

"No, it's not that. There are things about the city I love, and I want you to know that, to see it, too. I need to share it with you."

A pain shot through his stomach. He held it back, his eyes locked into hers. It was a golden day, and he wouldn't change that. It would be Mary's day.

"Come here, Mike," she said, stretching a hand out to him. "Come stand by me and look."

He pulled on his jeans, then walked over and stood beside her at the window. The street outside her window was alive with activity now, filled with honking horns and figures zigzagging between cars to cross the street, with delivery trucks and police cars and people going places in a hurry. Everything moved. There were several teenage boys gathered around a fire hydrant near the corner, their feet tapping out rhythms on the pavement, their hands moving as they eyed each female passerby with careful attention.

"What does all this mean to you, Mary?" Mike asked. He leaned slightly forward, his hands braced on the windowsill, his shoulders hunched. The window draft washed across his bare chest.

"What does it mean to me . . . ?" She thought hard, her brow furrowing. "It means a lot of things. It means life...teeming life. It means possibilities. I don't know, Mike—" She stood quietly, her eyes scanning the activity. "What I love isn't really what's right out there in front of us—it's what it all stands for." She turned her head to look into his eyes. Her face was serious, thoughtful. "Do you understand?"

"I'm not sure—tell me more."

"This city is so opposite Pinewood Falls where I spent all those years of my life. Everything here is possibility. From here you can go *anywhere*. You can become a part of the world any way you want. From Pinewood Falls you couldn't go anywhere, be anything. I was there with my father, and I was nothing. Nothing. I couldn't ever be anything there. It was stifling, Mike!"

The emotion in her voice was fierce. Mike looked at her with great tenderness, but there was nothing he could say. She was held captive by it, whatever *it* was, the feelings about her home, the life she had had to lead, her father. For some reason it was controlling her life. She probably was not even aware of it, but it was.

THEY SPENT THE AFTERNOON visiting a small art gallery that Mary loved, eating gyros at a dumpy out-of-the way place where the cook called Mary by name and welcomed Mike with a mighty slap on the back. At Rockefeller Center, they stood with their arms around each other and looked down on two skaters skimming across the white ice.

Mary looked at Mike. "Someday, Mike, we'll come back and do that together."

And then it was time to dress for dinner. A limo would be sent for them, Mary told him, barely disguising the excitement in her voice.

Mary's dress was emerald green, a silky, flowing gown that matched her eyes. Mike swallowed hard when she walked into the living room. "How much time do we have?" he said in a ragged voice.

But Mary barely heard him. Her heart skipped a beat and her eyes consumed him. She knew without any doubt that no man had ever looked so incredibly desirous, so handsome... but no, handsome was inadequate; it didn't begin to describe him. Mike's elegant black tuxedo fit to perfection. He was Adonis, David, her Michael, more startling and more striking than all the figures of history combined. She walked over and laid one finger along the side of his carved jaw.

"Watch it, lady," he said.

"I am.... That's the problem."

ONCE THEY ARRIVED at the hotel, the night passed by in a flurry of introductions and speeches and flashbulbs. Mike was sitting next to Henry Capra, Mary's agent, and he found the older man to be a wealth of gentle humor and intelligence. He liked him immediately. "Mary is lucky to have you," he said. "It's nice to know she's in such good hands."

"I was about to say the same," Henry said. And then he pushed his chair back from the table, puffed on his cigar and looked at Mike carefully. "The lady's in love with you, you know that?"

Mike was taken aback. He half smiled. "You don't beat around the bush."

"Why? What good did that ever do anyone or his brother? I just want the record straight. You love her?"

Mike took a deep breath. If he didn't like the guy so much, he'd punch him out. "Yes," he said, "I love Mary."

"Why does that sound like the dog died?" Circles of blue cigar smoke drifted around the man's head.

"Sorry. It's complicated."

"Yeah, isn't it always, except in those Fred Astaire movies."

"Sometimes it's more so than others."

Henry shrugged. His tuxedo cummerbund pinched around his middle when he moved. "Not a whole lot in life that can't accommodate itself to love." Then he laughed, a deep rolling kind of laughter that made others at the table nod his way and smile, too. "Damned if I don't sound like a romantic fool—imagine!" he said.

Mike laughed, too, forgiving the man his brashness.

"So...you have plans?" Henry persisted.

A flurry of activity behind them saved Mike from answering. A photographer wanted a picture of Henry with Mary and her editor for the next week's *Publishers Weekly*. Henry snorted, snuffed out his cigar on the dessert plate and slapped Mike on the back. "I like you, Mike. You'll do right by her."

And then he was off to stand by Mary's side, his heavy arm draped over her narrow shoulder. Mike watched them for a minute. Mary was radiant tonight, her cheeks flushed, her eyes as bright as he'd ever seen them. There were several other recipients of awards, but none held a candle to Mary, if only for her unbridled joy at being acknowledged this way as a writer. There was no false modesty, no pretense of it not mattering. It *did* matter to her, and anyone who looked into those gorgeous green eyes knew that. Mike found himself smiling at the power of the connection between them. He knew by looking at her what she was feeling, what thoughts were running through her head, what emotions were flip-flopping inside of her. She looked over at him once, and he knew in her glance that the same thing had happened to her, the same uncanny understanding.

Before the evening ended, the master of ceremonies made a final toast to the wonderful cache of new writers who had been brought together for the evening. At each of the round linen-draped tables, the writers were acknowledged one final time. The applause was thunderous and Michael squeezed Mary's hand beneath the table. He was as proud at that moment as he had ever been in his life.

Mary leaned over and kissed him on the cheek. "Thank you, Michael," she whispered. "With you here tonight, it's perfect—"

"Ms. Shields?" A young waiter stood just behind Mary's chair. As she pulled away from Mike, he stepped into the small space and presented her with a huge bundle of long-stemmed roses. Michael had almost forgotten about wiring them, but the look on Mary's face when she realized whom they were from was something he would *never* forget.

"No," she said, "I was wrong." With tears in her eyes she hugged him tightly. "*Now* it's perfect."

The next morning Michael was up first, and when Mary, groggy and with tousled hair falling across her eyes, shuffled into the small kitchen, he was there, dressed and humming.

"What's this?" she asked, her sleepy eyes caressing him. "Little Michael Sunshine. No one hums in this kitchen before noon."

Mike pushed her hair from her face, kissed her soundly, then held her quiet. "Okay, famous writer, yesterday was your day, today is mine."

Mary grinned.

Mike looked at his watch, then back at her. "You have eleven minutes for a shower, five minutes to get dressed, and thirteen minutes to enjoy a leisurely breakfast of—" he glanced behind him at the counter, then looked back at Mary "—of toast, jam, coffee and one hard-boiled egg."

"I can't dress in five minutes. Could I shorten the shower and breakfast and add to the dressing time, or—"

Michael silenced her with another kiss. "There. Don't mess with the schedule. It's been carefully worked out and any deviations might just ruin the whole day. Now scoot—"

He spun her around and gave her a slight nudge toward the bathroom, then stood there with his hands in his pockets as he watched her walk away.

He had been up for three hours, standing at the narrow living-room windows watching the world wake up below him, and thinking about Mary. Henry Capra's words filtered in and out of his thoughts—*you'll do right by her,* the outspoken agent had said. What were the alternatives? Michael wondered. Hell, he would do anything for her, do anything not to hurt her, that was a given. He would do right by her if it was the last thing he did on earth.

And as he had watched the activity begin, an idea came to him, something he could do that would be right for Mary, something that had been niggling at the back of his mind for a long time now.

"Michael," she said a while later, "this is crazy. Why won't you tell me where we're going?"

"It's an adventure."

They were speeding north along the New York Thruway in a shiny green Bronco Michael had rented from Avis.

Mary frowned. "There are so many wonderful things to do in the city—we wouldn't have even needed a car. There . . . there were so many places I wanted to take you, Michael."

Michael kept his eyes on the road. "I know, Mare, but trust me, this will be good, too. Alone in the car, just the two of us, no interruptions except the beauties of nature rolling by. Hey, it'll be great—"

Michael had checked the map earlier; it would take several hours, if traffic were normal. They stopped for coffee at a small diner, stretched their legs on a lovely wooded trail, and Mary finally relaxed. She was silly to turn Mike's visit into a tour of New York, she agreed. This was much better, just being together. They'd have plenty of chances to discover New York.

It wasn't until they had turned off 87 and onto a two-lane country road that wound through the Adirondacks that Mary realized where they were headed.

"Oh, no, Mike!" She sat forward in the seat, her hands on the dashboard. "What are you doing?"

"This is more important to me, Mary, than seeing New York. These are your roots."

Mary grew silent, but Mike could see her hands curling into tight fists.

He reached out and laid one hand on her thigh. "Mare, I . . . Maybe I should have consulted you first, but I knew you would have tried to talk me out of it.

And I wanted to come here, I wanted to see Pinewood Falls."

"Why?" she said simply.

"Because it's a big part of you, whether you will claim it or not. It still holds you, Mary—"

"No, I'm free of Pinewood Falls. I never looked back—"

"I think, my love, that that's the problem."

Mary finally looked at him. "No, Mike, there's no problem. But we're here, so I'll show you around Pinewood Falls. And then we can go back to New York. Henry would like to take us to dinner. Maybe we can get back in time for that."

"All right," he said, and slowly drove into town. He followed the sign that said Main Street, waiting for Mary to take the lead.

"What do you want to see?" she asked.

"Anything. Everything. You guide, I'll drive."

"All right, then, let's get this over with." Her words were clipped, but she wasn't angry, and for that Mike was grateful. "Turn up there," she said, "then right on Suwanee Drive—" She looked out the window at the quiet, picturesque neighborhoods. Nothing had changed, it all looked the same. Everything was exactly the same—

Mike followed her directions. He could feel her relax slightly, give in to the situation.

"Now slow down, Mike, there, that's it." She pointed to a tasteful brick house set back from the street. There was a circle drive in front and five huge maple trees stood on the front lawn. "That was my house," she said simply.

Mike pulled up in front and idled the engine. "It's a beautiful home."

She nodded. "I was the envy of all my friends. I had the best house." The words were spoken without emotion.

"Who lives here now?"

"I think Miss Sheehan, our housekeeper. My father left her some money. She used it to buy the house from the estate and as far as I know she still lives here."

"Shall we see if she's in?"

Mary started to shake her head no, but Mike was already out of the car. "Come on, Mary, I bet she'd love to see you."

Before they reached the door, it opened. An elderly lady, her gray hair piled into a haphazard knot on the top of her head, stood there looking at them. She wore thick glasses which she moved with one hand, as if that would bring them into clearer focus.

"Hello," she said cautiously, and then suddenly her face changed. Her eyes widened, her thin brows lifted and the beginnings of a smile tilted the corners of her small, pinched mouth. "No..." she said softly. "No..."

"Hello, Miss Sheehan," Mary said quietly. Mike glanced quickly at her. There was little emotion on her face.

"Mary, oh, Mary—" Miss Sheehan pushed the door open wider. Her thin arm reached out and touched

Mary, then gripped her arm and urged her inside. "Come, come in. I can't believe it's you—"

Once inside, Mary introduced her to Mike, but Haddie Sheehan paid little attention to him. It seemed astounding to her that Mary Shields was standing there in front of her.

Finally they moved into the large living room where Haddie insisted they sit while she made them tea. She served it in small cups on a large silver tray along with blueberry muffins. She was nervous, Mike could tell, but thrilled to have Mary there in her home.

"I've followed you, dear," Miss Sheehan said. "I know about your writing, your success. It's wonderful."

"Yes," Mary said. "I am becoming successful now, Haddie. Finally."

"You were successful here, dear," Haddie said quietly. "You were the most faithful, caring daughter a man could have had. And Lord knows that man didn't deserve the likes of you!"

"Haddie!" Mary said sharply. "How can you say that? My father was a wonderful man, he deserved everything, he—"

Haddie rose from her chair and came to sit beside Mary. She placed one blue-veined hand on Mary's knee. "Yes, dear, he was a wonderful man to the world. But he was awful to keep you here the way he did."

"Haddie—"

"Hush, let me talk, Mary. I loved your father for forty long years, I have a right to say this. He was a wonderful doctor, the world's finest doctor, but he never ever got over your mother leaving him—"

Mary's mouth dropped open. "No, Haddie, you're wrong—"

Haddie's arm was around Mary's shoulders now and she continued to talk. "He never told you because he was everyone's most magnanimous protector, but he was wrong not to tell you the truth. And I told him so, time and again. Your mother went off with another man, Mary, and your father never forgave her. He vowed early on that no one would ever do that to him again. And you, my sweet Mary, you suffered for that."

Pain squeezed Mike's heart. He wanted to go over and take her away, protect her from this. He wanted to wipe away the tears that were wandering unchecked down her cheeks. But mostly he wanted her to hear, to face whatever conflicts were driving her all these years.

Mary looked at Haddie. "He needed me—"

"He didn't need you that way, Mary. All he needed was your love. That's all. But he was so afraid to let you go your own way, so afraid you'd never come back, that he kept you here to care for him. Made you think it was the only way he'd get better."

"But it was right—"

"No, Mary, it was wrong. It was dead wrong. He saw your talent, he knew you should be going to school, being challenged, writing—"

"He saw my talent?"

"Of course he did. Your father was a brilliant man. And he was so proud—"

Mary stood. "No," she said, shaking her head, "he wasn't proud. I tried and tried to make him proud, but he never said, he never—"

Haddie reached for a book on the table. It was an old scrapbook. She opened it up. "Look, Mary."

Through her tears, she looked down while Haddie slowly turned the pages. There, carefully matted in the leather book, was every essay she had ever written. "He had me keep this, had me carefully save copies of everything you ever wrote. Oh, yes, my dear, he was proud. It was only his fear of losing you that prevented him from telling you. He was stubborn and selfish, but he *was* proud of you, and he did love you, more than anything in the world."

"He never...not once—"

Mike stood now and went to Mary, folding her in his arms. He wiped away the tears and held her until her body finally stopped shaking.

Haddie Sheehan stood and looked at the two of them. Then she said, "All right now, you two, stay put. I'll get us some more tea, and then I want to sit with Mary beside me, and see for myself what a fine young woman she's become."

IT WAS THREE HOURS later when Mary and Mike finally left Haddie Sheehan's house. She had insisted on fixing them sandwiches and would not allow them to leave without two boxes full of things that she had saved for Mary, things Mary had left for trash pickups or Goodwill when the house was closed, but which Haddie Sheehan had wisely confiscated and set aside for the day Mary would come back. There were albums, pictures in frames, toys, small art pieces Mary had made in school.

"I knew you'd come, you see. I knew the writer in you would bring you back, make you face all this, Mary. You needed to do that so you could walk away with the love, leave the anger and bad feelings aside."

"But—"

"Oh, yes, dear, *I knew* you had bad feelings, even toward me. *You* wouldn't admit it because you were such a good daughter, but you were angry, angry at the town, at all of us who were a part of the life your father built for you, angry at Robert Shields at the same time that you loved him so terribly. And he never gave you the space to sort them all out, so they stayed there inside of you like a tangled ball of yarn."

"Oh, Haddie, I'm sorry—"

"Sorry for what? Don't be silly, child. There's no room for that here. You had a tough row to hoe, you did. And look at you, you've done it. You're the finest young woman a dowdy housekeeper like me could ever have hoped to help raise."

Haddie Sheehan's eyes were damp when they left, but Mary promised faithfully to write, and she would come back, she promised. She would come back with a light heart next time, and good memories—

Mike was exhausted. He hadn't known what they would find in Pinewood Falls, but he knew Mary needed to be free of the demons that were born there. There were more demons, however, than even he had expected. Mary's mother, for one. Haddie told her that her mother had died very young; she and the young man she ran away with were killed in a plane crash. When he had heard about it, Robert Shields insisted on paying for the funeral.

For a long time, as they drove slowly through the hilly pinewoods country, Mary rested her head against the seat back, her eyes closed, and was silent.

It wasn't until they were back on the Thruway, caught in traffic, that she spoke. "Mike," she said, her head rolling sideways so she could see his profile.

"Hm," Mike said.

"I love you," she said softly. "I love you for today, for yesterday, forever—"

Mike reached over and took her hand. He felt drained. His own emotions were raw, thrown out there to the cold wind, whipped and ragged. Every minute with her seemed to deepen his love. And every minute in Pinewood Falls made it more clear to him how free Mary needed to be to move ahead into the future. There was no way he could ever, not in a million years, saddle her with the kind of life he had to offer. It would destroy their love.

Beside him Mary began to speak. Her voice was dreamy, slow. "Last night," she said, "during the awards presentation, I thought of my father. I thought,

'Dad, maybe now, maybe this will do it.... Are you proud of me at last?' ''

''You'd been driving yourself to make him proud. He chained you during life and he was doing it from his grave.''

''Because I was so angry. All I ever wanted from him was acknowledgment, pride. I think I knew he loved me, but—'' Her voice broke off.

''Now you're free, Mary. You can move on, succeed, but for Mary, not for your father, not to prove anything, not out of anger.''

She squeezed his fingers, wove her slender ones through his and closed her eyes again.

Finally, as the bright sun began to slip from the sky and the day's events began taking their rightful place in the background of her mind, she slept.

Chapter Thirteen

Dinner with Henry Capra was raucous and wonderful. He took Mary and Mike to a small Italian restaurant, and between the violin trio, the backslapping friends, clients and relatives that paraded past their table, many joining them for a while, and Henry's endless collection of publishing jokes and anecdotes, the evening rolled by on a wave of laughter and fun.

It was just what the doctor ordered, Mike thought, then smiled inwardly at the thought. Maybe there was a doctor at work here; maybe Dr. Robert Shields was finally easing things for his daughter, Mike thought; maybe at long last he was doing what was right for his daughter. All Mike knew for sure was that he could use a little help, and if it came from a man deceased for five years, that was okay with him. He'd take what he could get.

Every time he looked at Mary, his heart expanded, and then the tight pain came down with a crushing force that caused him to hold back, to order another drink, to try to distance himself. It was good he had come to New York, good he could see Mary in this world in which she was so comfortable. She had good friends here, friends Mike knew would watch out for her. That was good, he thought, nodding absently. She'd be fine. And even the awful part—knowing without any doubt that Mary could never marry him— was good, because at least there was the cleanness of certainty.

"Mike?" Mary said beside him. "Are you okay?"

"Righter than rain," he said, and then smiled crookedly. "I never knew what the hell that meant."

Her hand was beneath the table, resting on his thigh, and now she squeezed it lightly and Henry filled in the space with another story, another punch line that called for laughter. Healing laughter, Mike thought. He wasn't sure what that meant either. Mary had only revealed a little bit about their day to Henry, but it was enough for Henry to take Mike aside and tell him if he ever needed a favor, Henry was the man to come to. "Mary's like my own family. What you did today," he said, his flat gray eyes locking into Mike's, "was worth blood. She needed to be free of all that garbage. You helped her do it and I'm grateful to you for that. You remember that."

"Just take care of Mary," Mike said, and then he turned and walked off, returning to the loud group that had joined their table, and leaving Henry staring after him as if he had spoken Greek.

Mary was dancing with another of Henry's clients when Mike returned to the table and he was glad. It was easier watching her from a distance, memorizing all the lovely things about her. When she was close to him the pain was greater. He could feel it moving in, ready to blacken out his soul. He stared down into the highball glass. Damn! Why had he let it go this far? Why had he let himself fall in love with her? The liquor had weakened his control and he could feel the tears stinging his lids, could feel the power of the emotion that was building up inside himself. Before anyone could notice, Mike shoved his chair back and left the room. He slipped out the front door and into the cold black night.

The restaurant was on a busy street lined with small shops, restaurants and offices. He walked briskly, going nearly a full block before he realized he had left his coat back at the restaurant. An icy breeze whipped around his legs and he wrapped his arms around himself, rubbing his arms brusquely. Without conscious thought of where he was going or why, Mike stepped off the curb to cross the street.

A screech of tires and loud shouting pushed him back until he hit the curb, stumbled, then fell back onto the pavement.

There was a man standing over him now, an angry, cursing man shaking a fist. "What the hell do you think you're doing? Walked right in front of me, you crazy drunken fool! You could have gotten yourself killed!" The man's face was red and angry and he looked about to kill Mike himself, when a strong arm pulled him away.

"You okay, mister?" said another voice and the angry driver backed off then, cursed again for good measure, and got back into his car. With the smell of burning rubber lingering above the asphalt, he sped on down the street.

Mike looked up at the man who had helped him. "Yeah, I'm fine," he said, pulling himself up. "Thanks. I didn't see him. Didn't see the car. Stupid. So damn stupid."

"Yeah, we all get in a cloud now and then," the other fellow said, then walked on down the street.

Mike stood there for a minute, staring at nothing. He had not seen the car. He had hardly seen anything. The lights, the cars, the fuzzy figures on the streets. Night blindness, John Seaver called it. It would come and go. Mike lifted his head to the sky. And then he took a long, stabilizing breath, cursed the anomalies of fate, and walked slowly back to the restaurant.

"YOU WERE SO QUIET, Mike," Mary said as she readied herself for bed. Mike was lying on top of the covers, completely dressed, watching her. He had been watching her all night, and when she caught him at it, the cold river of fear would snake through her until she blotted it out, forced it away with all her strength.

"Mary," he said softly, "I have to leave early tomorrow. My plane leaves at eight-thirty."

"We'll change it and go back together. I leave at noon—"

"No, Mary."

The words were heavy, ominous, and Mary walked over and sat down on the side of the bed. "Mike, what's wrong? All night, there's been some kind of undercurrent, something wrong. I haven't asked because I didn't want anything to ruin this, to—"

"But you know it, too, Mary. It's not going to work."

"Mike, you're frightening me. We were going to talk this weekend. Talk about our future. I love you Mike. I don't know how we'll work this all out, but we will. I *love* you."

Mike took both her hands and held them still. "Mary listen to me. We can't. It isn't going to work—"

"Do you love me, Mike?" she asked suddenly. Her eyes flashing, challenging him.

Mike didn't look away. He watched the gold flecks, dancing now, deep sapphire flecks against the emerald sea of her eyes. "Mary, I love you more than I ever thought I could love anyone. You're a part of me. And that's why—"

Mary pulled her hands away and covered her ears. "No, Mike, don't say it. I won't hear it—" The fear was overwhelming now, a bruising, powerful force that was squeezing the breath out of her lungs.

"Mary you have to listen—"

"Mike, if we love each other, it will work out. I know how you love Indiana—" She was talking fast now, speeding her words along so there was no time for Mike to say anything, so there was no time for the fear to grow any larger. "We could spend time there each year—summers, maybe, or fall when it's so lovely. And Mike you're like I am, we're birds of flight, you can lecture here or there, I can write anywhere. Paris, Spain, the world is ours, Michael, together, you and me—"

"Mary, please stop." Mike wondered where the calmness had come from. It fell down upon him now like a giant blanket. It spread out over him and settled each nerve, each thumping of his heart. He held her hands again and looked deep into her eyes. "No, Mary, you'll have to fly alone. I can't—"

"Mike, stop!"

"I can't stop, Mary. And you have to listen to me."

"We can make it work." There was desperation in her voice, the pleading of a child.

Mike looked at her, his eyes filled with an incredible sadness. He shook his head slowly. "Mary, it won't work, the two of us. I can't see the world with you. I can't be a bird of flight. Mary..." He paused for just one second, and then he finished, finally. "Mary," he said, "I'm going blind."

Chapter Fourteen

She did not move. Her whole body was still.

"Mary—" Mike didn't touch her. He sat still on the bed, reaching her with his voice, thick now with sadness and regret. "Mary, I think somehow there was another way to do all this, but I don't know what it is."

"Michael," she said, her hands rolled into fists and pressing into the softness of the mattress, "explain to me what you are saying."

Michael watched her, saw the beginning fingers of pain working their way into her eyes, her voice. He had caused this. He had caused the one great love of his life this great, enormous pain, and there was no way to turn back. He had to plunge ahead until the reality of it all swallowed her whole. "It's called retinitis pigmentosa. There isn't any cure for it. The severe results may not occur for some time. Or they may occur tomorrow."

Mary looked at him now with a calmness that was unnatural. She folded her hands in her lap. "How long have you known this, Mike?"

"For two years."

"Two years—"

"I...I had some blurred vision and had some tests run when I was home at Christmas that year. Andy was just beginning his studies and I did it more to humor him than anything else. Once we knew, once *I* knew, then I started figuring out what I'd have to do, how I'd live—"

"This is why you came back to Indiana to live. The job in maintenance, that whole facade—"

Her eyes were flashing now. A deep flush coated her cheeks. Suddenly it occurred to Mike what was going on here. She was angry. No, she was not angry, she was mad as hell!

"I'm not sure what you mean by facade," he said slowly.

"That whole damn thing! Not telling me about the teaching position, the Harvard degree, everything!"

Michael stared at her. He was startled, not sure what to say next. He was prepared for disbelief, sadness, tears. But not this, not this overwhelming anger that darkened her eyes like an Indiana storm cloud.

"Mary, I'm sorry, I—"

"Sorry? You're sorry?" She leapt off the bed and stood beside it, glaring down at him. "Sorry for letting me fall in love with you? Is that what you're sorry about? Or sorry about deceiving me? Tell me, Michael, what are you the sorriest about?" She pounded her fists into the bed until Michael thought the stuffing was going to come out.

And in the next moment, before he had a chance to move, her strong, lovely body, straight and elegant as a ballerina's, crumpled into a heap on the floor, and with her head buried in her hands, she began to sob, a terrible, gut-springing sound that tore Mike's heart into a million pieces.

He got up from the bed and went to her side but she brushed him away. She never looked up. "Please," she murmured, "please leave me alone for a while."

Mike walked from the room and closed the door softly behind him. He looked around vacantly, then grabbed his jacket and left.

There was a faint flurry of snow in the air when he walked out of the apartment building, but Mike barely noticed. He was wiped out, drained, and every inch of his body ached. The distance he walked never registered, nor the cold, not the scattered vagrants who eyed him warily as he shuffled by. It was not until a police car pulled up alongside him and asked him if he needed help that Michael turned and slowly walked back to Mary's.

He had planned his future so carefully, worked out the kind of life he would have with the skill of a systems analyst—how could he have handled this so badly?

He passed the diner, then rounded the corner and crossed the street to Mary's apartment building.

He didn't see her until he was up close, almost to the front door. And then she moved, and his eyes slowly adjusted, taking in the figure huddled against the wall behind the glass doors. She had an old blanket wrapped around her and all Mike could see were her eyes, as large as the moon, sad, tender eyes the color of a grassy field.

She pushed the door open from the inside, and when he walked through, she took him in her arms and clung to him as if there were no tomorrow.

With their arms wound about each other, they made their way upstairs.

They sat on the couch with cups of hot tea in front of them, untouched. Talk came slowly and with great effort.

"Mary," Mike said finally. "I'm so terribly sorry. I did this all wrong. The whole damn thing."

Mary shook her head. Any movement started the tears again and she pressed herself into Mike's side as if that would stop them. "It's too much, Mike. So many emotions are shifting around in me, strangling me— I feel like I'm drowning. But you, Mike, what must *you* be feeling?"

She looked at him so tenderly, so compassionately, that Mike felt he was sinking. He didn't want this, didn't want pity or sympathy. He'd been through all that. Her earlier anger was far easier to deal with.

"Mary," he said slowly, "let me lay it all out for you, and then you'll understand. I never talked to you about this earlier because there was no reason to. I don't want people's sympathy. I've dealt with this in my own way, it's handled."

Mary listened to his words, but what jarred her was the excessive firmness of it all, the set to his jaw, the threat in his voice that said, 'Don't mess with it, because if you do, if you shake it, everything may fall apart.' "There's an enormous difference between sympathy and understanding, Mike," she said.

"Not a lot, Mary, not in my experience. Anyway, I came back to Indiana because I knew I'd have a better life there— I never liked the world of high finance anyway. It was too fast, too pressured. I'm not like that and I missed the time to enjoy life. So it was a decision triggered by the disease, but something I would have probably done at some point anyway. I asked Bill to take me on in maintenance because I wanted to do something with my hands, to develop skills. I wanted to know every inch of the campus before my sight failed me. And I wanted some time to think it all through—"

"That's what you robbed me of, Michael—"

Mike looked at her sadly. "Yes, I did. The difference was that I didn't know I was going to fall completely in love with you until it was a done deal. And then it was too late."

Mary looked down at the table. Her head hurt, and her heart was squeezed so tightly inside her chest she wondered how it could still work. She was struggling so hard to handle all this, to put everything in its place, and to make good and proper sense out of it. But emotions battled against reason and all she wanted to do was have Mike wrap her tightly in his arms and tell her it would all be better in the morning. But when she looked up into his clear blue eyes, she knew with startling clarity that he was not going to tell her that.

"Michael," she said slowly, "you said this might not happen for a long time..."

"Yes." His voice was quiet.

"We can deal with it."

"Mary, I can deal with it. But you can't."

"Michael, people with impaired vision marry, have children, lead fruitful lives."

"Yes they do, love, and I will have a fruitful life. There will always be one great sadness in it now, but I'll have a decent life."

She looked up, her eyes filled with tears. "Why are you doing this? Why are you pushing me away? Do you think there's any way I would let this destroy my love for you? Don't you know me at all, Michael?"

Mike drew her to him then, wrapped her tightly in his arms. He could not bear to look at her face, to see the great pain there. "Darling," he said softly, "I took you back to Pinewood Falls for me as well as for you. I needed to see for myself what your life was like there. And I saw it, almost as though a video player were highlighting moments for me. I saw what eight years of caring for your father did to you. And no matter what you think or say, I know without a doubt that you'd come to feel the same constraints, the same binding shackles, with me. You wouldn't want to, but you've been through too much already, Mary—there've been too many scars."

A shiver ran through Mary's body and into Mike's fingers. Along with it came her anguish, and it flowed directly into his heart.

"You're wrong, Mike—" she said, her voice ragged.

"Mary, I love you too much to let it happen. I love you more than I could ever imagine loving anyone. And if we married, if we built a life together and I became totally blind, you'd feel it, the constraints, the feeling that you needed to devote your life to me. And I don't want that Mary. It would destroy our love.

"You need to be free to do all the things that are flung out there across the world for you. You need to taste them, play with them, and I know you, my darling, I know you like my own soul. Whatever you think now, however we tried to work it out, you'd begin to feel enslaved. No matter how independent I tried to be, you would feel the duty, the obligation, just like with your father—" He kissed the side of her head, then caught some of the tears that were rolling down her face with the tip of his finger. She was shaking her head no, denying his words, but Mike knew; he had had weeks to think about it, and he knew.

Mary curled her body into his side and tried to assimilate everything he was saying but the emotions were too large, too preponderant, to allow her thoughts to form. All that was real was that her world was falling apart and she seemed powerless to stop it. She closed her eyes, let Mike's fingers work their magic on her shoulders, her back. And finally she drifted off, knowing it was all a mistake, a horrible mistake; Mike was here beside her, holding her, loving her, the greatest love of a lifetime. Together they were invincible. Nothing could destroy this, nothing.

BUT WHEN SHE AWOKE in the morning, she was lying on the couch, covered with a thick blanket. And the apartment was as still as a tomb. She knew before she stirred, she knew before she opened her eyes, that Mike was gone.

The letter was near the coffee machine. He had perked a pot of coffee for her, then stuck the letter beside the carafe.

My dearest Mary,
I've had the luxury of time, and that is what you need now, my love. You need time to assimilate it all, and to allow the truth to come into your mind and your heart.
I've never loved like this, Mary, and I never will again. It's a gift. We've been given this great love, darlin'. Some people never have that, not even for five minutes.
I will carry you forever in my heart.

                                                            Mike

HENRY CAPRA DROVE MARY to the airport later that day and tried to console her as best he could. "He loves you, Mare, that's why he's doing it. It's a damn shame, but sometimes love is fated this way—" He hugged her tightly, then pulled out a large linen handkerchief and shoved it into her hand. "If there was any way I could make this right, Mary, I'd do it. I'd go talk to the guy myself, but I know how much he loves you, I know it from last night. And this is the only way he can deal with it. This is what he thinks is best for you."

"But he's wrong, Henry, damn it! He's dead wrong."

Henry handed her suitcase to her. He looked at her sadly. "Maybe he's not wrong, Mare. Maybe he's not—"

SHE HALF EXPECTED to see Mike at the airport in Indianapolis, his crooked grin warming her heart and telling her it was all a bad dream. But he was not there, and the long limousine ride to Chestershire was agony. She had held herself in check on the plane, giving in to the anger she still felt, but now, as the terrain took on a familiar look, as memories flooded back and she saw Mike everywhere she looked, the tears began to fall again. She could not imagine being without him. Could not imagine life without him.

She walked into her bungalow and dropped her suitcase on the floor inside the door. And then, without thought or planning, she went to the phone and dialed Mike's number. If they talked some more, surely they could work it out. Somehow.

But there was no answer. Nor was there any later that night, nor the next day. Finally, in desperation, Mary summoned up all her courage and called Marie Gibson.

Marie answered on the second ring and Mary held back her tears and introduced herself.

"Of course, Mary dear, how are you?"

"Mrs. Gibson—"

"Please, dear, call me Marie. I feel as if you are part of the family."

"Marie..." Mary's knuckles were white from gripping the phone. She began again, "Marie, I wonder..." But her voice would not work. The words could not get past the lump in her throat.

"Dear, Michael isn't here. I know that's why you're calling."

"He's not at his house—" Her voice broke again but Marie graciously ignored it.

"No, he isn't, Mary. He's in California."

"California...?" She could barely get the word out. She could feel it starting all over again, the tears, the pain, the terrible emptiness opening up.

"Yes, Mary. He's on the board of a company he used to own out there and there was a meeting. He doesn't always go, but he decided at the last minute— he called us from the airport in New York. I thought he would have told you—" Her voice trailed off.

"No, he didn't mention it. Will...will he be back tomorrow?"

Marie said nothing for a minute. Then she spoke softly but with great kindness. "Mary, I'm sorry to tell you this. Michael should have told you himself. It was wrong of him not to, and not like him, at all. He will be in California for two weeks.''

Two weeks! Mary's heart fell. Two weeks...she would be gone in two weeks. He was staying away until she was gone.

"He has a place out there," Marie went on. "A beach house. When he moved back to Indiana he sold everything else, but he hung on to this place. He always thought it would make a nice vacation house someday. A good place for kids. But he's changed his mind, apparently, and he thought he'd stay on after the meeting and try to sell it.''

"But—" The tears were coming now, an endless river. Mary felt them blurring her vision, lying cold on her face. She couldn't speak.

"Dear, I don't know what to say. But I'm here. If I can be of any help to you, come to me.''

Mary nodded, tried to speak but couldn't.

Finally Marie suggested they hang up for now, "but," she told Mary kindly, "please remember that I'm here, dear. And I suppose I know my son as well as anyone—''

MARY THREW EVERY OUNCE of energy she had into her workshop. And for those hours each day, she survived. The only feedback from the students was that she looked pale, and they continually offered her pills from their stashes of Vitamin C. If only Vitamin C could do the job, she thought, if only a simple pill would fill the horrible ache that was in the very center of her being. But nothing could ease that, and the time away from the workshop became an empty, hollow void, a time that had been filled with Mike—and now there was nothing.

This was it, then. This was what her life without Mike would be, a hollow, gray existence. She walked over to the gazebo after class and sat on the wooden bench, the wind whipping her hair around her face, and she felt nothing. Would she ever feel anything again? She looked up at the gray sky. A winter sky, she thought, a sky that matched her soul.

Polly came over that night, bringing chicken noodle soup. She sat in the dimly lit living room holding Mary's hand and listening carefully to the whole long story.

When Mary was through, Polly gave her a fresh box of tissue, and then she began to talk, slowly, calmly and carefully. "He loves you, Mary," she said. "That's all I know for sure. This other—this feeling he has of ruining your life, I don't know about that."

"He sold me short, Polly," Mary said.

Polly's voice was gentle and soft. "He doesn't see it that way, honey. He could be right about what would happen, you know, and you need to think carefully about that. You had some difficult years being tied to someone who was very needy. Mike has never planned to let anything limit his independence, and he's a remarkable man, so in most respects it won't. But at its worst, there are some things that would be affected, *real* things, no matter how much everyone wants to deny them, and Mike knows that. He knows there will be situations at some point in his life others will have to help him with—''

"Of course there will," Mary said, her thin shoulders sagging, "Isn't that true of everyone? Don't you and Stu depend on each other for things?"

"Sure we do, Mary, but not in the same way. Not in the same dramatic way. But I've known Mike for so long and I know his ending things with you is more than surface stuff, Mary. Sure, you'd do things for Mike, sacrifice for him simply because you love him, whether there were handicaps involved or not. But this goes deeper. It's because of all you're bringing to this, Mary, that Michael is so fearful of you. It's because of those years in that little town in upstate New York. It's because of a vivacious young girl who gave up her youth to care for someone. It's because that beautiful young girl does not deserve a repeat, and somewhere along the line, in some unknown year flung out there in the future, Mike is afraid that that's exactly what you would be feeling. And there isn't any way on earth he would allow that to happen to you. Don't you see that, Mary?" She locked her eyes into Mary's, forcing her to listen, to think about what she was saying.

"He's your best friend, Mary," Polly went on, "and he knows better than anyone about your plans, your goals, and the life you have mapped out for yourself. And that's *not* Mike's life, Mary, not even remotely so."

She leaned her head to one side and looked at Mary with great affection. "You and Mike have such a special love, Mary. And it's because it is so, that Mike is doing this. Whether he's right or wrong, he's doing it out of love."

When Polly left, Mary was exhausted. Her head throbbed and every bone in her body ached. She played with each thought, stretched it out in front of her, tried to attend to it, but finally her mind and body gave up. She shuffled into the bathroom, stripped off her clothes and stepped into the hot shower. For a long time she stayed there, scrubbing herself, holding her head back so that the steady stream of hot water sprayed down her face, washing the salty tears away. Much later, when the room was filled with steam, she got out and rubbed herself dry. And then she wandered through the house, searching for the thick old robe that Mike had worn that very first night. She held it for a minute, rubbing the fleece against her cheek, and then she dropped her towel and wrapped her body in the robe. With her feet bare and the lights on, she curled up in front of the fire, cradled in the smell of him, the lovely, musky smell of intimacy, until finally, much later, she slept.

"MARY, YOU DON'T LOOK so hot," Stu Tolliver told her a few days later. Their paths had crossed in the middle of campus when Mary, her head down as she walked aimlessly along the path, walked into him.

"No, I'm not so hot, Stu," she said. "But I'll get better. I don't seem to have a choice, do I?" An edge of anger bit into her words, and as she tasted it, she liked it. It was such a refreshing change from the days and nights of pain and sadness.

Stu noticed the life in her eyes. "Hey, now *that's* the girl who plays outfield like a pro! Where there's a spark, there's a chance for fire. Come on, Mare, this calls for a cup of coffee."

He wrapped one arm around her shoulder, stopped traffic with the other, and directed Mary across the street from campus to a Donut Heaven.

Mary sat across from him, and for the first time in a week, she felt blood in her bones. "Stu, this has been the longest week in my life, and I'm ready for it to end."

"I'll tell you, Mary, I'm for that. You look like hell. I talked to Mike last night, he *sounds* like hell. Now what kind of a world is it when two people who really care about each other are miserable?"

"You ... you talked to Mike?"

"Yes."

"How ... is he?"

"He's crazy in love, Mary, that's how he is. He's miserable, what do you think?"

Mary was silent. She stared into her coffee cup.

"He's pigheaded as hell, but he's a special guy, Mary."

"Listen, Stu, can't you be a real friend and tell me he's a worthless jerk?" She stared at him helplessly, her eyes round and sad. She could not hang on to the anger; try as she did, it never seemed to last. "I want to be mad at him. He's done this, he's made this horrible decision, and he's left me—just pushed me out to live my own life." Her voice caught, but she struggled on, her sad eyes searching Stu Tolliver's face for an answer. "And the thing of it is, Stu," she said, her voice growing soft, "I can't figure out how I'm going to live without him."

"Then don't, Mary," Stu said, and he got up, leaned over and kissed her on the cheek. "Don't do it, Mary. It's your life, after all. Now, I'm late for class. I'll do my thing, you go and do yours."

THE ANGER CAME BACK later, shortly after she had gone to bed. Mary welcomed it, got up, paced back and forth, and cried out to Michael in the middle of the cold, drafty kitchen.

"Why, Michael? Why have you sold me so short? Why have you decided for me what my future will be? What *right* have you to do that? What right, Michael?"

And then her voice broke off, and the pain came back in terrible rolling waves, and without another word, Mary curled herself into a little ball and burrowed beneath the blankets of her bed.

But by the next morning Stu's words had taken root. Eight days, she thought. She had survived eight days without him. She had grieved and been angry and cried until there were no more tears. And she was sick of it.

This was her life, too, and the only person in the whole world with full responsibility for it was herself. He was wrong, that was all. She had listened and thought and analyzed, and in the end, she knew with total clarity that Michael Gibson was absolutely, unequivocally wrong.

The thought brought a smile to her face, and then out of the blue she was crying again, hopeful tears that lit up her face and sent her scurrying to the telephone.

Chapter Fifteen

Professor Atwood received the first phone call and he was as accommodating as Mary had hoped he would be.

"I'll only miss two days, Professor," she said, "and the students are all set to spend those days critiquing each other's works. They'll never know I'm gone. Then I'll come back and wind things up. Oh, and Professor?"

"Yes, my dear?"

"I'd like to do another of these real soon. Let me know if you're interested."

Professor Atwood told her he most assuredly was, and Mary hung up and crossed the first hurdle off her list.

Between calls to the airport and one to Polly and Stu to tell them her plans, Mary called Marie Gibson. She would be at Mary's door in thirty-five minutes, she said, and then she added with a sparkle in her voice, "with bells on!"

Mike's mother was true to her word, and she hugged Mary tightly when she arrived, then hurried her out to the car. "You've a plane to catch, young lady," she said in an exuberant voice. "Let's not tarry."

The flight to California was endless, but a week of sleepless nights had taken their toll, and finally, as the plane soared smoothly over the Rocky Mountains, Mary slept.

The next thing she knew a stewardess was shaking her gently telling her that all seats needed to be returned to an upright position. The San Jose airport was ten minutes away.

Before picking up her rental car, Mary went into the rest room and splashed cold water on her face, ran a brush through her hair and smiled into the mirror. So what if she looked a little haggard and worse for wear; she'd been through a damn war, she might as well look the part!

The thought that there was one more battle left sent a small trickle of fear down her spine, but she straightened up, forced it away, and walked briskly out of the rest room and over to the Avis counter.

Minutes later she sat in the car, scanning a map and the addresses and phone numbers Marie Gibson had given her. Mike would be at the beach house, Marie had said. It was the place he loved the most in California. She thought selling it was ridiculous, and had told him so, but Mike seemed adamant on the idea, and being as stubborn as his father, there was nothing she could say to him.

Mary rolled down the window. It was a perfect California day, sunny, brisk, blue skies. She allowed herself a long, stabilizing breath of California air, then slowly eased the car from its parking space and out onto the open road.

MIKE WAS STANDING at the deck of the house, his hands pressed into the railing, his eyes scanning the sea. He had finally become accustomed to the sunglasses and they made his long walks along the shore, with the sun turning the sand a glistening white sheet, comfortable.

God, he was tired. Bone weary. Far off in the distance a sailboat skimmed the uneven waters, its sail puffed out and only the tip of the hull visible behind the waves. Mike envied the sailor, knowing the vessel was demanding every ounce of his attention, every muscle of his body, every fiber of his being. That was what he needed, something to consume him completely, something to black out the pain, to pull him into another level of consciousness, to rescue him from the pain that lay unmovable at the bottom of his heart.

He shouldn't have stayed out here at the beach house. Bad planning. Dani had laughed when he had bought the place a few years ago and wondered what they'd ever do with such a place—a place with a long dormitory room filled with bunk beds on the top floor, with a built-in trampoline in the small square of lawn on the side, with a homey living room and large sunny kitchen. There was even a boat house with water skis and surf boards, and a dog cottage that was built to match the main house. "This is a place for kids, not adults," she had said. And as if to sink its fate for good, she mentioned that it wasn't a fashionable spot, no guard at the gate, no photographers lurking behind cars trying to take furtive snapshots of famous residents.

She was right, of course. And that was why Mike loved it: he knew immediately, when he came upon it that day, that it was everything he wanted. It was a place for kids, for a family. A vacation spot to get away from city life, pressures, people; a place to spend time together playing ball and running the beach.

It was right to sell it, he thought now. Absolutely right. The house represented everything he wanted to have with Mary, everything that was impossible. She'd love this place, he knew. She'd love everything about it. There was even a small den with a window that framed the sea, where she could write...

God, how he missed her! He hadn't counted on the rawness, the feeling of exposure, as if every nerve ending were right out there, subject to the elements. And he hadn't counted on each day being as bad as the one before. Books and songs told you it got better, but it didn't. He guessed the writers had never met Mary. The raw ache was there when he went to bed and it was there when he got up.

"Hey, big fella..."

And now he was hearing her soft, slightly husky voice inside his head as substantially as if it were beside him. He shook his head, as if to blur the voice. He was losing it now, he really was.

"I *said*, hi, big fella..."

He half turned then, just enough to see the flash of red shirt, the sweep of dark hair, tousled by the ocean breeze. He made a sound, from deep in his throat.

"Not much of a welcome," she said. Her eyes were bright with unspilled tears.

"Oh, Mare..."

She took a few tentative steps toward him. "I...I took one look at this magnificent place, and I knew exactly where you'd be— I knew there'd be a deck on the back that stretched out to the sea, and I knew you'd be here, on the edge of it, looking out—dreaming those dreams of yours—"

Mike stared at her. He could not trust himself to speak.

Mary tilted her head slightly and nibbled on her bottom lip. The tears began to move slowly down her cheeks but she made no move to catch them, to hide them behind a sweep of her hand. "You sold me short, Michael," she said calmly.

"Did I?" he said. She stood ten feet from him, but he could feel her, feel the flat plane of her back, the warm, tender press of her skin. His breath caught in his throat.

She nodded. "Yes, you did."

"Could you...could you come closer and tell me about it? Because if you don't I'm going to lose my mind."

Mary smiled softly, and then, with the back of her hand, she brushed away some of the tears and moved across the deck. "We can't have that for you're going to need every bit of that feeble mind of yours to process what I've come to say to you."

But once she touched him, once Mike's hands slipped behind her neck and his fingers threaded through her hair, the talk was put on hold.

"I never thought I could love like this," Mike said when Mary finally pulled away, her face smudged with tears, her eyes bright.

"Well, that's good," she said, then sniffed and demanded a tissue. "You've had a screwy way of showing it lately, but maybe we can work that out."

"Mare—"

"No, my love, hush." She pressed her fingers against his lips. "It's my turn now. Last week was yours, this one is mine..." She looked up at the face that had never, not for one blessed moment, left her mind, and said, "Who knows? If you behave yourself, maybe next week will be ours."

Mike had drawn her down into an enormous rope hammock that stretched between two poles on the side of the deck. Her body was pressed wonderfully into his and her feet dangled over the side.

Mike shifted his glasses to the top of his head and gazed at her face, at the small mole at the side of her cheek, the freckle on the tip of her ear. He had never noticed the freckle before and now he found it enchanting. How many other things were there about her that he had not yet discovered?

And then the familiar ache crept in. Fate . . . the enemy, the maker of impossible unions . . .

"Michael, the truth of it all is that I love you."

Mike took a long breath. "That's a given, Mare—"

"No, no, it's not. These things need to be lined up for you, it seems. Your love, Michael Gibson, has made me more alive, more open to the world and every blasted thing in it, than I have ever been in my whole life. For days now, I've gone over it all in my mind. Oh, the feeling was there right off— I knew immediately that you were crazy to walk away the way you did. I knew we belonged together as surely as I knew my name—but I needed to line everything up, to see it all brightly and clearly and not just emotionally." She stopped and took a breath.

Mike was silent. Inside of him a giant weight, repressive and awful, was lightening, lifting—

"I need you, Michael," she said. "I need you desperately. You've helped me rip away from these things in my past that were shackling me, holding me down, and then . . . and then you leave—" Her voice, so strong a minute ago, began to break.

Michael held her closer. He couldn't bear to see the sadness in her face again. "Mary, it's okay. We can talk later, we can—"

"No, we can't!" The strength was back, and Mary plunged on. "You're so logical, so orderly, and plan everything so carefully, but you didn't allow something in all that, Michael. You didn't allow me to grow. I *see* now what my father did. He was handicapped in a way far more awful than you'll ever be, Michael. He was sad and fearful and couldn't allow me to live my own life because of that. And I was so angry after he died, so terribly angry, but I never knew why. And I attacked life in a way I thought would make up for it all. You helped me see all that, you helped me understand it. My father loved me, but not in a healthy way, Michael. It was oppressive. How can you possibly—'' her voice rose now and the tears began to flow more profusely ''—how can you ever in a million years think you're like that? You are not my father, Michael. You are my best friend, my lover.''

She took his head between her hands, and with her tears spreading to his cheeks, she kissed him fiercely. And then she held him slightly apart and she choked, ''And now, Michael, now will you be my husband?''

Michael regarded her for a long moment. The brightness and love in her eyes was nearly blinding. And then he gathered her into his arms and pressed her tightly to his chest.

''Does that mean yes?'' she said, her words choked and strained.

He wiped the tears away from her cheek with the back of his hand. ''I don't know. What kind of dowry do you have?''

''Want to see?'' she said, and the playful, bright specks of gold began to dance in her eyes, and then Michael knew, without a doubt, that Mary was back.

HOURS LATER THEY SAT drinking champagne on the deck, their glasses clinking together in a giddy, unbounded celebration of their love. The sky was midnight blue and scattered stars blinked in the distance.

"I'm not naive, Mike," Mary said, her hand resting in his lap. "I know there are a lot of things to work out. I want to keep my apartment, for starters."

"In New York?"

"It's rent-controlled. Can't give that up," she said. "And it will make working with Henry and my editors convenient. And besides Mrs. Corcoran, the little lady on One, thinks you're just about the sexiest thing to hit Manhattan."

"She's right, of course."

"Of course." She kissed him again. "And then there're the kids—"

"What kids?"

"Ours. Something else I had never given much thought to until I met you, I think because I wasn't raised in a traditional family."

"Mary, you're moving so fast," he laughed, "I can't keep up—"

"I have absolutely no doubt in my mind that you'll keep up, Michael Gibson!" She laughed with him now, and the sound was familiar and sweet to his ears.

"I think I want you all to myself for a while— I need at least a year to make up for this week—"

Mary nodded happily. "And then, sometime . . . do you think I'd be a good mother, Mike?"

"Absolutely. The best. How many kids?"

"Let's negotiate."

"Yeah, negotiate." His arm went around her. "I like negotiating."

"But not tonight. Tonight's special."

"And tomorrow?"

"Tomorrow we go back to Indiana. And begin negotiating."

Michael took her hand and drew her out of the chair and toward the house. "I can't, darlin'. A buyer is coming to look at the house. I may need to sign some papers." He had almost forgotten about the realtor's call. Having Mary here had turned the world so blissfully upside down.

"No," she said sweetly, her arm looping around his waist.

"No?"

"If we're not here, then it can't be sold. A shame—" She looked around at the beautiful oceanfront home, and then back at Mike. Her eyes were moist. "But think of it this way, darling, we've a ready-made honeymoon spot."

"Do you think," he said, his voice thick, "it would be appropriate to have an early honeymoon housewarming?"

"I think it would be lovely," Mary answered.

And he picked her up in one smooth movement, and carried her across the threshold of their lives.

Take 4 bestselling love stories FREE

Plus get a FREE surprise gift!

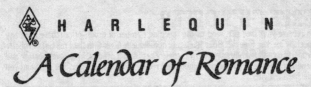

HARLEQUIN

A Calendar of Romance

Be a part of American Romance's year-long celebration of love and the holidays of 1992. Celebrate those special times each month with your favorite authors.

Next month, we salute moms everywhere—with a tender Mother's Day romance.

**#437
CINDERELLA
MOM
by Anne Henry**

Read all the books in *A Calendar of Romance*, coming to you one per month, all year, only in American Romance.

FREE GIFT OFFER

To receive your free gift, send us the specified number of proofs-of-purchase from any specially marked Free Gift Offer Harlequin or Silhouette book with the Free Gift Certificate properly completed, plus a check or money order (do not send cash) to cover postage and handling payable to Harlequin/Silhouette Free Gift Promotion Offer. We will send you the specified gift.

FREE GIFT CERTIFICATE

ITEM	A. GOLD TONE EARRINGS	B. GOLD TONE BRACELET	C. GOLD TONE NECKLACE
# of proofs-of-purchase required	3	6	9
Postage and Handling	$1.75	$2.25	$2.75
Check one	☐	☐	☐

Name: _____

Address: _____

City: _____ State: _____ Zip Code: _____

Mail this certificate, specified number of proofs-of-purchase and a check or money order for postage and handling to: HARLEQUIN/SILHOUETTE FREE GIFT OFFER 1992, P.O. Box 9057, Buffalo, NY 14269-9057. Requests must be received by July 31, 1992.

   PLUS—Every time you submit a completed certificate with the correct number of proofs-of-purchase, you are automatically entered in our MILLION DOLLAR SWEEPSTAKES! No purchase or obligation necessary to enter. See below for alternate means of entry and how to obtain complete sweepstakes rules.

MILLION DOLLAR SWEEPSTAKES
NO PURCHASE OR OBLIGATION NECESSARY TO ENTER

To enter, hand-print (mechanical reproductions are not acceptable) your name and address on a 3"×5" card and mail to Million Dollar Sweepstakes 6097, c/o either P.O. Box 9056, Buffalo, NY 14269-9056 or P.O. Box 621, Fort Erie, Ontario L2A 5X3. Limit: one entry per envelope. Entries must be sent via 1st-class mail. For eligibility, entries must be received no later than March 31, 1994. No liability is assumed for printing errors, lost, late or misdirected entries.

   Sweepstakes is open to persons 18 years of age or older. All applicable laws and regulations apply. Sweepstakes offer void wherever prohibited by law. Prizewinners will be determined no later than May 1994. Chances of winning are determined by the number of entries distributed and received. For a copy of the Official Rules governing this sweepstakes offer, send a self-addressed, stamped envelope (WA residents need not affix return postage) to: Million Dollar Sweepstakes Rules, P.O. Box 4733, Blair, NE 68009.

ONE PROOF-OF-PURCHASE

To collect your fabulous FREE GIFT you must include the necessary FREE GIFT proofs-of-purchase with a properly completed offer certificate.

(See center insert for details)